POT LUCK

by
David L. Gersh

Published by Open Books

Interior design by Siva Ram Maganti

Cover images © Aleynikov Pavel shutterstock.com/g/pavlintiy

© miniwide https://www.shutterstock.com/g/miniwide

ISBN-13: 978-1948598453

For my dear friend Elaine, whom I lost this year. I had a terrible time here with "who" or "whom". Elaine would have known.

And to Anne, as always.

Chapter 1

MY PANTS WERE STIFF at the knees with Willy's blood. The metallic smell didn't seem to bother the Sheriff. It sure bothered me.

The sun was settling comfortably into the trees for a long night's rest. Sheriff S.A Patera and I were sitting in Willy Witkowski's backyard. The police technicians were packing up their gear.

Heat was starting to flee. A nice deputy found my jacket. I threw it around my shoulders.

Sheriff Patera was a pert woman of about forty-five with black, short hair, licked with gray. She had alert eyes and a lively mouth. She didn't look like a police officer. Except for her starched brown shirt and her big gun.

She flipped open her notebook. "Mr., um..." she scanned her notes, "Harris." She paused thoughtfully, then smiled at me showing a lot of white, even teeth.

"I know your name from somewhere, don't I? Wasn't there some other murder you were involved in? Chief Carsone mentioned something, but I didn't quite get it."

I wouldn't say involved. No, certainly not involved.

"Janet Mason," I said.

"Ah, yes. I remember it now. It was before I came here. You also discovered that body."

I nodded, but not happily.

"You're a lawyer, aren't you, Mr. Harris?"

1

"Yes."

"She was your client?"

"Yes."

Then she pivoted. Thank goodness. I certainly didn't want to talk about Janet Mason.

"How well did you know Mr. Witkowski?" Her voice was nonchalant, almost indifferent.

"I've known Willy... I mean I knew him, for several years. He was a good client."

"Oh, he was your client too?"

"Yes."

"And you discovered both bodies?"

"Yes."

Who's counting? I know I wasn't.

"Were you personal friends with Mr. Witkowski?"

"I handled several matters for Willy over a number of years. Which I'm not at liberty to discuss. But I like to think of myself as a friend to all my clients."

"Mr. Harris, why did you come to see Mr. Witkowski today?"

"I needed to talk to him about some business matters."

"Legal matters?"

"No, business. We worked together."

"You worked with Mr. Witkowski?"

"At Wee Willy's."

"That's the marijuana company?

"Correct."

"How long have you worked at Wee Willy's?"

"About three weeks."

"What kind of business matters did you need to discuss?"

"I needed to talk to Mr. Witkowski about money we needed in the business."

"I see. How was the business going, Mr. Harris?"

"There were some issues."

"Money issues, I take it."

"Yes."

"Did you know about these money issues when you gave up your legal practice to join the company?"

I hesitated. "Not exactly."

"Were you angry with Mr. Witkowski?"

I didn't like that question at all.

"Well, I wasn't overjoyed with Willy. But if you are asking if I was so upset, I killed him, I didn't."

———————

You may be getting the wrong idea about me here. Perhaps I should explain.

Chapter 2

MY NAME IS JAMES Emerson Harris, and I'm a lawyer. Or, at least, I was the last time I checked. I read the disciplinary section of the State Bar report first thing each month. Call me paranoid.

But I am the second smartest lawyer in San Buenasara. I'm sure you've heard of me. It may not sound so impressive to be the second smartest. But my junior partner, Clyde, is the smartest, so we've got it covered.

My once and future wife, Karen, is smarter than both of us, but she's not a lawyer, thank goodness. Karen and I were divorced by accident but I'm working on that. It wasn't my fault.

Bruno doesn't count. I don't mean one-two-three-four. I mean he's not included, although if he were, I think he would contend he is the second smartest. Bruno's our dog. Actually, he's Karen's dog, a beautiful long-haired dachshund. He tolerates me.

I hope Karen loves me more than she loves Bruno. I think so. I have to say it was a little disconcerting when I asked her to marry me again. She had to check with Bruno first to see if she could get a better offer.

I guess I need to explain my relationship with Karen. It may seem a little confusing. But it's absolutely normal.

Back a few years ago, I fell off the wagon. Leaped actually. I was under a lot of pressure.

Karen and I had been married three years. We lived in L.A.

and one of my sleaze-ball drug-dealer clients, Manny Comacho, objected to my efforts on his behalf. I got him a corner cell, the ingrate. He was sending me threats, which was not so new. But the last one had been sent to Karen. She went nuts. And I went nuts.

Karen is a strong-willed lady. She left for San Buenasara and she gave me the chance to join her if I cleaned up my act. But she wanted to make a point. So, she got this shyster in San Luis Obispo to file for legal separation. The jerk couldn't even check the right box. It's a printed form, for Christ's sake.

He checked the box for divorce, not separation. I must have missed it. To tell you the truth, I don't remember seeing it. But, I don't remember much from those days.

I did get sober and seven years ago I moved back in with Karen. That's when the divorce became final.

We had a good laugh about it. Karen was lying back against the cushions on our sofa and I was sitting on the floor by her feet, my cheek resting on her thigh. A glass of white wine was perched on her stomach. I was sipping my O'Doul's.

It was late on a Sunday afternoon. The sun was already low in the sky. We had a little fire going in the fireplace. The wood crackled and the dancing flames were hypnotic.

Karen is a beautiful woman with a lithe body and small perky breasts which I admire as often as possible. Her red hair is just starting to show a little gray. She has it cut in a pixy style. At least I think that's what they call it.

Her eyes are this unbelievable light green with golden flecks, and she has freckles dusted across her nose. She thinks she is as tall as I am, but I'm sure that's just envy.

I'm a tall five feet, seven inches and forty-five years old now. My blond hair is turning gray, but it hasn't dimmed my boyish blue eyes or my lopsided grin. Age has not been as kind to my hair. It's thinning to the point where I'm thinking of negotiating a better deal with Sal, my barber.

I gave Karen my best smile. I don't do it very often and never in my car. Women going in the other direction have been known to crash.

I told her I would file to have her lawyer's egregious mistake corrected. I may have directed some impolite terms towards him.

Karen got this mischievous look in her eyes.

"I don't think so," she said with a little half-smile on her lips.

"You don't think your lawyer is a schmuck?"

"No, I don't think we should have the judgement vacated."

I was a tad taken aback. I turned my head and looked up at her.

"We have a great relationship. What are you talking about?"

"Of course we do. I love you." She scrunched up her nose.

"I love you too. Don't you want us to be together?"

"Yes. I just don't want to be married."

"Are you crazy?"

"Yep."

I did the only practical thing. I went to my mother to convince Karen to let me get the judgement vacated. Karen really likes my mother. My mother looked at me appraisingly. Then she refused.

We've gone on living together. Our relationship is the same as before. She's my office manager. We work together every day. And sleep together every night. Over the last seven years I've asked Karen to marry me at least five times that I can remember. The best I've ever gotten out of her is, "Maybe."

Until last New Year's Eve. In a weak moment, she said, "Yes". After attempting to solicit an offer of marriage from Bruno, as I've mentioned.

Never have so few done so much for so few.

Chapter 3

IT WAS A BEAUTIFUL Thursday in late August. Karen and I were having breakfast at The Lilly Pad. The Lilly Pad is the best restaurant in San Buenasara.

I had finished my coffee and poached eggs. I hate poached eggs, but Karen was watching. Personally, I believe a little weight looks good on a man. Karen agrees. Our problem lies in defining "little."

I was wearing my favorite cowboy shirt with the pearl buttons. I think it looks great with my ostrich leather boots and pressed jeans. Women were surreptitiously admiring me as we ate. They kept dropping their forks.

We walked out the door into the sunshine. It must have been a frigid 68 degrees. It had been a cool summer. A hint of an ocean breeze touched my cheek. The air smelled of seaweed and salt. I lifted my head and closed my eyes. It was one of those perfect moments. I turned to Karen.

"God, this is beautiful. I wish it could last forever." She looked up at me with a worshipful smile. I'm a towering five feet, seven inches, but I can tell when someone is looking up to me. She appreciates my innate sensitive nature.

"That's what I love about you, darling."

What insight the woman has.

"With you, a perfect morning seems longer."

We were just at the door of our little house where we live and practice law. I was still trying to figure out whether Karen had complimented me or put me down when our receptionist, Pamela, burst through the door.

Pamela isn't as concerned about her weight as one might be, so bursting was a pretty good verb for what occurred. She looked anxiously in the wrong direction. But she got it right on the second try.

"There you are. Thank goodness."

"Hi, Pamela. What's up?"

"Judge Hendricks called."

"You mean her clerk."

"No, she called herself. She wants you in her court right now. I think she's angry."

"What makes you think that?"

"Well, she called you a whole lot of names. And her voice was squeaky."

"Tell Clyde to go." Clyde is my junior partner. What are junior partners for, if not to talk to angry judges.

"She wants you."

"Did she say why?"

"No. She just said it real loud."

———

Karen poked her head around the door. I had just gotten back to the office from my visit with Judge Hendricks and had settled into my chair. I knew I had settled in because Bruno jumped into my lap and made himself comfortable.

I had swiveled my chair to look out over our small marina. The one where topless young ladies often serve as deck hands. Not that I have ever seen one. Even with the binoculars I keep in my desk.

I turned back quickly when I heard Karen come in. Bruno jumped off my lap, giving me a wounded look. He waddled over to Karen, who kneeled down to scratch him behind the ears.

I'm a strong man. I suppressed my jealousy. And my desire to bark.

She finally came over and sat down in one of my client chairs. She crossed her legs. She was looking over my shoulder.

"We really need to get that crack in the wall fixed." She turned her head. "And this room could use some paint."

Our little house was built about 100 years ago and remodeled the last time to install electric lights. It always needed something fixed. We should burn it down and start again.

"As soon as we can afford it."

She shrugged and recrossed her legs. I really like to look at her legs.

"What was Judge Hendricks so mad about?"

"Her honor seems to feel that I am screwing with her calendar. My motion to delay the Witkowski trial doesn't seem to have pleased her."

"Why did you file for the delay?"

"We haven't completed our depositions."

"You haven't taken any depositions."

"That's why we haven't completed them."

Karen closed her eyes and her lips were moving in silent prayer. It's what happens when you are in the presence of genius.

Willy Witkowski used to be our local bookmaker before he went straight. Straight into selling illegal controlled substances. You have to give him credit though. He had the best pot in town. Not that I would know. I've been sober for years. But he had great reviews.

I first met Willy about five years ago after he was arrested at the San Luis Obispo Airport for indecent exposure. No, Willy isn't a pervert. He's a stoner.

He was on his way to Denver, looking down at the world from on high. He was standing in the TSA line waiting to go through the metal detector. A young man asked him to take off his shoes and belt. Willy's a nice guy. He wanted to be cooperative and stay ahead of the game. He was arrested as he was trying to drop his boxer shorts.

The D.A. was laughing so hard Willy got off with a slap on the wrist. I got a good client.

Between Willy's marriages and divorces and his brushes with our esteemed criminal justice system, I thought about giving Willy a volume discount.

Now I'm Willy's personal and business attorney. Willy is five feet, four inches and as thin as a broom. He's bald with scruffy tufts of hair at the back. Pencil necked and with a thin face, he looks like a squirrel. No offense to squirrels. Everyone calls him Wee Willy.

When California legalized pot, Wee Willy really did go straight. He received the only growing and dispensary license in San Buenasara.

Here in San Buenasara, we are on the cutting edge. We have the best of Berkeley and Chicago rolled into one. Seven thousand happy souls, most of them high. And we are politically correct. We don't have manhole covers. We just passed a law to rename them maintenancehole covers. How's that for gender sensitivity.

And our marijuana industry is thriving. After Willy discovered our city council couldn't be bought, but that it could be rented, he applied for a license. It was a highpoint for our elected officials. Most of them were high at the time.

It turned out Willy was quite the businessman. He bought a greenhouse from Francis Hendley who had an old farm up in the hills, and started growing marijuana in at least four strains. He hired a lady to do the packaging and marketing. She had retired from a major advertising firm in Los Angeles. Then, he had a company down in Santa Barbara begin manufacturing CBD ointments and creams. CBD is the medicinal stuff in pot. A food company was making whoopee brownies, cookies and butter. Butter?

Wee Willy's was on everyone's lips, particularly if you bought the lip balm. Its products were sold through weewillys.com in every state where it was legal. Don't ask me how he made delivery.

At the end of last year, Wee Willy's had formed a joint venture with a company called Campboll Water to acquire an eighty-acre hemp farm about ten miles up the coast from here. Hemp doesn't have a lot of the stuff that makes you high, but it does have a lot of CBD.

Between the sales in San Buenasara and his internet business, the money had to be rolling in. Willy was living high. I mean "well." And well, "high." But he seemed never to have a lot of money. I guess he had a lot of expenses.

Chapter 4

Karen looked at me and cleared her throat. She has a great attention span. I tend to wander. Now Bruno was looking at me quizzically.

"What?" I said.

"Okay, I'll bite? Why haven't you taken any depositions in Willy's case?"

"They cost money." That gave Karen pause. Her eyebrows lifted and her nose wrinkled as she sought to absorb that wisdom.

"Explain."

"Look, this claim only involves $25,000. After Willy bought his new Ferrari, he noticed a spot on the finish. He thought the car should be repainted. Tom Maji, the owner of the dealership, disagreed. So, Willy hired us."

"And?"

"Maji knows we can't spend a lot of money. There's never an attorney's fees clause in this kind of deal, so we can't ask for our costs. He's working us."

"You seem to be helping."

"Not at all, my dear. We are engaging in, what we call in the higher realms of the law, strategy."

She was waiting on pins and needles. It must have been uncomfortable. Nonetheless, I paused a moment to allow my full brilliance to light the room.

She tapped her fingernails on my desk. Bruno glared at me.

Karen gave me the dirty eye.

"Come on, Jimmy."

I cleared my throat.

"In a lawsuit for $25,000, we don't have any leverage. We needed to create some. I filed the lawsuit to let old Tom know we were serious, but I never intended to pursue it. What I did do was name Ferrari of North America as an additional defendant on a product defect claim."

Karen smiled; a glorious thing.

"Then I called the president of Ferrari North America. I spoke to his nice secretary. I asked her why they would market a defective product."

"Okay."

"It took about thirty minutes for the general counsel to call me back. I explained the issue to him in great detail. I reminded him that Willy paid $382,000 for the car, in cash. I also let him know how important and how influential Willy was."

"You lied."

"Yes, but I did it really well. You would have been proud of me. Now, I am simply waiting for the regional sales manager of Ferrari of North America to put the arm on Mr. Magi."

"And why will they do that?"

"Ferrari is coming from a different place. They, of course, don't want any inference that they are selling anything but perfection. Tom, on the other hand, doesn't want any problems with Ferrari. He needs them. Voila.

"I am expecting a call from Tom in the next day or so, asking what color we would like and if he can polish the fuel injectors. I will ask him to also pay our modest fees. Whereupon, I will dismiss my lawsuit."

Karen applauded. I modestly bowed my head.

Chapter 5

IT WAS ANOTHER BEAUTIFUL morning. Perhaps a bit brisk. Brisk here is down to 58 degrees. At the end of the block, small waves were lapping the beach. The blue stretched out to the horizon. I loved the idea of living inside that thin black line on the edge of the map of the United States. I was humming to myself as I walked down towards my office with a full tummy. French toast is a nice way to start the day.

For years we rented the house where we have our offices and home. It's a little, frame, two-story house painted a pretty pastel yellow. There is a tiny front lawn and a white picket fence in front. Karen has planted white roses against it. Some are still in bloom.

We bought the house last year during a brief period when we were flush. That hadn't lasted long. Business had been dreadful. But we're two blocks from the ocean and four blocks downhill from Main Street. That's important because The Lilly Pad is on Main Street.

I've mentioned, haven't I, that Karen is a wonderful, talented woman. But among her many sterling qualities is not cooking. It's not that she couldn't. She just doesn't want to. I respect that, probably because I don't want to be beaten up. Call me a coward.

So, Lilly, of Lilly Pad fame, feeds me breakfast every morning. Then I power walk to my office. I'm all for discipline and exercise, but downhill after breakfast is good.

I strolled up our little concrete walk and opened the door. I always arrive first thing in the morning, around ten o'clock. Pamela was guarding the fort. She smiled at me.

"Mr. Witkowski is here. I just let him into your office." We don't have room for a lobby.

"Great." I had asked Willy to stop by. Mr. Maji, the Ferrari dealer, had called and I wanted to deliver the good news in person. I opened my office door to greet Willy.

No Willy. Then I looked down. Willy was lying face up on my floor.

"Hi, Willy," I said, with my usual unruffled aplomb. "Why are you lying on my floor?"

"I tripped," he said amiably. There was nothing to trip over.

"Are you okay?"

"Oh yeah. I just tripped over my feet." Willy was notoriously clumsy. Particularly when he was high. Which meant he was always notoriously clumsy.

"How long have you been lying there?"

"A while."

"Don't you want to get up?"

"I kind of like it here."

"Why?"

"I never noticed your beautiful ceiling before and I'm enjoying the view."

The view is out the window behind my desk. The ceiling is cracked and stained. I stepped over Willy's legs and made it to my chair. I sat down. I couldn't see Willy.

"Willy, you might get up now."

"Nope."

"Okay, I got a call from Tom Maji," I said, speaking to the empty air. "He wants to negotiate."

"Great. What should we do?"

"I told him we wanted the car repainted with sixteen coats of lacquer."

"Is he gon'a do that?"

"After he stopped yelling at me, he said he would. You've got to go over and select a color."

"How long's it gon'a take?"

"Not to worry. I told him you wanted his Ferrari to drive while yours is being painted."

"He gon'a do that too?"

"He was overjoyed to accommodate you, Willy."

———————

It was late the same afternoon. Willy had insisted upon celebrating. Karen, Willy, Bruno and I were sitting in a booth in The Lilly Pad. I was sitting with my back towards the wall, which is always wise for lawyers and gunslingers.

Lilly doesn't admit dogs. A Health Department thing. But we have all agreed that Bruno is really a very small person. I'm not sure Bruno fully embraces the downgrade, but he likes The Lilly Pad.

We don't let him sit at the table. He lies underneath it on Karen's toes. She always kicks off her shoes and tickles his belly.

Lilly had broken out her private stock of Zager Chardonnay and she joined us in toasting Tom Maji's abject surrender. She thought Tom was a pompous ass. I toasted with the best sparkling water in the house.

We were on our third glass when Lilly wandered off to talk to another regular. Karen went off to the restroom. Willy and I were alone. Well, Bruno was there, but he is always discreet.

Willy leaned forward and lowered his voice. His lips moved.

"Willy, I can't hear you. Can you talk a little louder?" I looked around. No one was anywhere near us.

Willy raised his voice a notch.

"Things are going great." He had animation in his face and his eyes were bright. "We're going to start dating each strain of marijuana we sell. And get reviews. A vintage kind of thing. You know, like they do with wine."

I never knew Willy was awake long enough to be good at business.

"We'll age some a few months. Our marketing people are nuts for the idea. We'll call it 'Wee Willy's Reserve.' They think it will open a new market at premium prices."

"Gosh, that sounds great."

"And we've got a new tagline. I tell you, I really like this marketing woman."

"Okay, hit me with it." I thought that was witty, given to whom I was speaking.

"Aim High."

"I love it."

Willy turned serious. "Jimmy, I got a problem."

"That's what I'm here for."

"Well, that's kind of it. What with marketing and the new lines and expanding production and, you know, quality control, I can't keep up."

Particularly with quality control.

"You do look tired," I said.

"I mean there's so much to do. So many decisions to make. The new farm, the greenhouses, pricing. I can't do it all."

I was missing something here.

"Gee, Willy, can't you hire someone to help?"

"I want you to be the president."

That stopped me dead. I was at a loss for words. For a lawyer, that is a real loss. And they weren't just lost, they were wandering in the woods somewhere.

"Well, uh, Willy, that's very flattering."

Karen came up behind me and put her hand on my shoulder. "What's very flattering?"

"Willy wants me to be president of Wee Willy's." I sounded incredulous, even to myself.

"That's a great idea," she said.

Well, damn. That gave me pause.

"But, what about our law practice?"

"Oh, Clyde does it all anyway," she said.

"Hey, wait a minute."

"And I handle the business end. We'll be fine." Et tu Brute?

"Yes, but..."

"And this would be a chance for you to stretch. Hone new skills. You've been getting bored a lot lately."

"Well, yes, that's true."

I felt my ego getting hard as she stroked it.

Willy interrupted. "We'll pay you $200,000 a year. Just like me. We have some little issues, but this is a great business."

"We could use some more money," Karen said.

Then Willy delivered the coup de gras. "We'll give you options on ten percent of the company."

Well, why didn't he say so before. I stuck out my hand.

"I like the idea, but it's a big decision. I'll talk it over with Karen some more and call you. Tomorrow or the next day."

I had no suspicion that Willy was so clever and I was so dumb. But I was about to find out. There were a few more questions I should have asked.

Chapter 6

KENNETH SINGER WAS WEARY. It had been two years since he had received a regular paycheck, and frankly, it was getting to him.

The pressure seemed to never let up. Elizabeth was carping about the alimony again and the kids schooling was bleeding him dry.

Wharton and the Harvard Business School were great credentials, but they didn't put bread on the table. Or, for that matter, wine in the cellar.

Kenneth looked at himself in the reflection of the floor-to-ceiling windows of his overpriced office. It was a great two room suite in the best business district in Boston. The decorator had done a first-class job. She should have for the money he spent. But he needed to make an impression. Wealth Management is a conservative business.

He got up and walked closer to the window to have a better look. He leaned in and pulled his bottom eyelid down. Bloodshot. Then he examined the dark patches under his eyes.

He looked like shit for a thirty-two-year-old guy, he concluded. He ran his hand through his thinning brown hair and sat down again. The chair squeaked under his weight.

Maybe he should never have left Morgan Stanley. His boss had been an arrogant asshole who had no clue about quantitative investing. And they had been shorting him on the bonuses he deserved.

His friends had left to set up their own shops and they were making big money. What had he done wrong?

He poked at his stomach. Christ, he was getting paunchy. That gym membership he bought in a moment of guilt would be a godsend if he ever got to use it. He wandered back over to his desk.

His grandfather had been named Schmindl. His dentist father had changed it to Singer when he started his practice in an old Polish neighborhood in Cleveland. He didn't think any of his patients would be able to pronounce Schmindl, much less write it on a check.

His solidly middle-class family had provided their only son with braces and a new nose. College and business school had dressed him impeccably. It had polished his speech to butter up the upper crust. So what was the problem?

Singer Capital Advisors had $60 million dollars under management. It just wasn't enough. He was making decent returns for his clients. Sure, they were a percent below the benchmarks, but he always told anyone who complained that he put capital preservation first. No one withdrew their money.

The problem was, no one increased it either and new clients were hard to come by. God knows, he was trying. And this was the longest bull market in history. He had to do something.

He was working to get a share of the Boston City Employees' Pension Fund. He'd paid enough in campaign contributions and eaten enough tough steak medallions to take three years off his life.

Now the chairman of the fund was nibbling around for a bribe. He didn't know if he would go there. He would cross that polluted river when he stood on its banks, and not before.

Sixty million dollars brought in $600,000 a year, plus or minus. But after rent on his showy office, fees, research costs and his rather engaging secretary, whom he hoped would learn computer skills one day, that left $350,000. And that was less than it cost to live well in Boston, even without alimony.

Or the deal he had had to make with the IRS after his last audit. That was costing him $6,000 a month. That annoyed him, but not nearly as much as having to send a check every month to that bitch of an ex-wife.

He glanced at his watch. It was late and he was hungry. He could use a drink. With a sigh, he pushed back from his desk and started to pack up his briefcase.

The phone rang. He picked it up.

"Singer Capital Advisors."

"May I speak to Mr. Singer, please?" an older woman said.

"I'm Kenneth Singer. May I help you?"

"Mr. Singer, my name is Agnes McKittrick." She sounded substantial. Singer perked up. "I'm the president of our ladies' investment club. And we are looking for an investment advisor."

Singer deflated even faster than he had perked up. Another bunch of bored grandmothers investing their pennies.

"Can you come meet us on Tuesday at teatime?"

"Mrs. McKittrick, may I ask how you came to me?"

"My attorney, Andrew Chase, recommended you. Mr. Singer, is there a problem?"

Andrew Chase was his classmate at Wharton and a partner in one of the most prestigious small firms in Boston. Well known for representing the Boston monied class.

"Oh, not at all, Mrs. McKittrick. I just like to know who to thank. I'm not sure I know when teatime is."

"We will meet at four o'clock, at my home." She gave him the address. It was in Chestnut Hill, an upscale Catholic neighborhood.

"Then I will see you at four o'clock on Tuesday. I look forward to meeting you."

Chapter 7

THE HOME WAS A substantial two-story, stone house set back on a hill and surrounded by about two acres of manicured lawns. Maybe these old ladies did have money. Even a small investment fund worked pretty well if they traded a lot.

He was led by a maid into an elegant dining room. The walls were paneled in mahogany that looked as if it had been polished daily for a hundred years. A crystal chandelier hung over the table and eight heavy upholstered chairs surrounded it. The table was covered in a handmade lace tablecloth. Agnes McKittrick sat at its head.

"You have a beautiful home, Mrs. McKittrick. And I love this paneling. Is that a Whistler?" he said pointing at a painting on the wall.

"How perceptive, Mr. Singer. A great grandmother on my side of the family. The story is that Mr. Whistler was a family friend in London and painted great grandmother as a favor to my great grandfather. He did a splendid job, don't you agree?"

"Yes. The painting is lovely."

"Do you enjoy art, Mr. Singer?"

"I do, although I'm a novice. But I loved art history in school." The Whistler was worth over a million dollars.

"Well, Mr. Singer, welcome. We use the small dining room when there are so few of us."

Quite. There were six other older women gazing at him expectantly. He recalled a retired Harvard professor talking about his first lecture on a cruise ship. He looked over his audience and thought the average age was dead.

Agnes McKittrick was a soft looking woman, in her seventies, a bit on the stout side. Well dressed and proper. She sat erect and her manicured hands lay flat on the dining room table.

Singer had done his homework. Agnes McKittrick was the widow of Sean McKittrick. "Big Sean," as he was known, had been in the heavy construction business and had been deeply involved in Boston politics. To his credit, not a single parking garage or tunnel he built in the last ten years had collapsed.

He had been powerful and, it was said, a very rich man. Unfortunately, Mr. McKittrick had passed away two years ago while spending a paid vacation at the invitation of the Federal government for going a gift too far.

"Please, Mr. Singer, sit at the other end of the table so we can all hear you clearly," Agnes McKittrick said with a smile and a gesture. She had vividly green soft eyes. There was something unsettling about them, like looking into the eyes of a doe reflecting off a campfire on a dark night. Something vulnerable and innocent.

"Thank you for coming, Mr. Singer. May we get you some tea? Perhaps a scone. The scones are made by my cook and they are exceptional."

"Thank you. But no. I'm fine."

She made introductions around the table, then lifted her hand to Mr. Singer.

"Ladies, Mr. Singer is an investment advisor who comes to us highly recommended. And he is Jewish. My late, dear husband always said you should have a Jewish accountant and a Jewish investment advisor. And, as you all know, Sean was very successful."

Except for that one small mistake. Singer bit the inside of his cheek so hard he could taste blood. Thank God it hurt so much he couldn't speak.

"I have chosen him to help us," Agnes McKittrick continued. The ladies all primly nodded their approval. One of them smiled and gave him a little wave.

"Mr. Singer, as I told you, we have made a decision to make some small investments. My friends and I hope to find it stimulating and, well, fun. Of course, and I must emphasize this, our privacy is essential. We are very private people."

"I do understand. That's not a problem. I can form a shell company in the Caymans for you. I have the contacts. It is a little expensive."

That might get rid of them. How bad was this going to be? Small investments?

"That is a good idea, Mr. Singer. Please see to it. Can you suggest a name?"

That surprised him.

"Uh, I've always fancied the name 'Eclectic.'"

"Oh, so do we!" She smiled and clapped her hands. "Don't we, girls? Our own Cayman's corporation. How exciting."

Now he was really confused. Were these people delusional?

"But Mr. Singer, we are older and risk averse. It would worry us to have too much invested in any particular company. Although, we do hope it will be interesting."

Yes, delusional. His hopes were sinking faster than a lead canoe.

"I readily understand your concern," Singer said. "My view is that capital preservation is as important as an adequate return." Best to get that in place up front.

"But you do understand that certain private investments require a minimum commitment," he continued. "Can you tell me what you had in mind?"

Maybe this was a way out.

"Well, Kenneth... May I call you Kenneth?" She continued without waiting, "No more than $6,000,000 in a single investment. I do hope that is enough."

"Oh, that should be sufficient." His voice had a strained quality. He coughed.

"May we get you some water, Kenneth?"

"No, no. I'm fine."

Mrs. McKittrick pursed her lips and tapped her fingernails on the table.

23

"Perhaps, Kenneth, I failed to make it clear that we do not want many funds or stocks. What we want is to invest in start-up companies where we can follow along. Make a difference." Her voice had a lilt and sounded like it slapped the table for emphasis.

Singer spoke hesitantly. "Mrs. McKittrick, that sounds like venture capital and venture capital is very risky."

"That is why we want to keep our investments small. We appreciate what you are saying, but we do want to have a good time. Are you aware of any start-ups that might interest us?"

Singer was so blindsided, his mind seized up. He grasped at a telephone call he remembered from the prior day with a friend in Los Angeles.

"Well, I did get some interesting information on a pot company."

Then, he realized what he was saying. He gave his forehead a mental thump. God, how stupid.

The woman next to him perked up. He thought she had been asleep. Or worse.

"Oh, Agnes. My Henry made a fortune in utensils. He loved utensils. He always said to me, you have to have a pot for every chicken."

"But..."

"Now Kenneth," Mrs. McKittrick said, "we mustn't interrupt."

Chapter 8

"JIMMY, CAN WE BE serious?"

"Sure, I'll even marry you."

She hit me. It hurt.

"I need something."

I knew she wasn't talking about sex. And I wasn't willing to bet she wouldn't shoot me if I brought it up.

"You know I'd give you anything," I said

She rolled over and put her hand on my shoulder. Her naked, small breast pressed against my arm. Maybe she was a lousy shot. Maybe we didn't even have a gun in the house.

I could see her face in the moonlight that was crowding into the room. There were tiny crow's-feet at the corner of her green eyes. And there were laugh lines on her face. They were our past and our future. I can't tell you why, but I was filled with a deep sense of joy.

"What do you need?"

"I don't know."

"That makes it more difficult."

"I know."

"Tell me how you feel."

I got that from a psychologist when I had my free State Bar rehab program. In truth, it is about all I remember of the experience. Of course, I am getting old.

"I feel empty. Like nothing I do matters. I have a big hole in me."

I know about feeling empty. Have the scars. I was experiencing a sense of restlessness too. I always did when I was afraid of starving.

But I wondered what had brought this on now? Karen was always so upbeat and full of energy.

Maybe it was because the practice was so slow. The country was in a recession. I know because I heard that on the news.

I never understood how a recession, caused by who knows what, could extend its grip and choke the life out of a little town like San Buenasara. Everyone was fretting. The motels, the small shops that sold postcards. Even Polly was complaining about the drop in adult toy sales.

Only this morning, Lilly was distressed about having to lay off a waitress. I couldn't remember when The Lilly Pad wasn't busy. But it wasn't busy now. And if I didn't get some more clients soon, I was going to have to start cooking my own breakfast. Or take the job with Willy.

"If you had to make a list, in order, of ten things you always wanted to do, at whatever cost, what would be on that list?" I asked.

She thought about that. I thought about her naked breast that was pressed against my arm. Hey, I'm shallow, but I'm lovable.

"Jimmy, you know I dropped out of college in my second year."

"Sure. You said you wanted to be out in the real world."

"That wasn't exactly why."

Karen and I had been together a long time. Most of that time had been spent trying to solve problems I had created. Or making love. We had never talked much about her past. I knew a little. Not a whole lot.

We had met in a bar in Hollywood. The usual happenstance. I was going on a date. It fell through. A guy friend suggested we go to this great bar. We meet a girl at the bar who had dumped me a few years back. She introduces me to Karen.

I needn't point out that Karen is beautiful. But I thought she was incredible. No one had ever focused that much energy on me. The concentration in her eyes just gripped me.

We talked for four hours straight. They closed the bar. All of our friends had left. We hadn't noticed.

That was fourteen years ago. I was a mature thirty-two. Karen was twenty-three. I took her home that night. I didn't even try to hit on her.

We moved in together two months later. I knew why I was there. I had no idea why she was. With all my bluster, I do have some self-doubt. Uh, forget I said that.

I had even less of an idea fourteen months later. We got married in a little park overlooking Lake Hollywood.

Things were great. The practice was good. We had money. Karen never wanted children. At least she never mentioned it. Was that what this was about?

"Okay, got it. That wasn't exactly why you left school," I said.

"Jimmy, I've never talked about it. To anyone. I'm ashamed."

"Darling, first, I'm not anyone. There is nothing you could tell me that would matter. Except, maybe, if you were really a man. Then we'd have to discuss it."

She hit me again. But at least she smiled.

"Whatever it is, whatever happened, tell me. I promise you I am ashameder than you are."

"My father was a drunk."

"You never talked about him."

"I had gotten into college on a full scholarship and I was working at night as a waitress to pay for my room and board. My dad thought it was a waste of time. My mom thought I should be bringing in money for her and the family."

"Your parents didn't approve."

"I wanted to be a doctor. It was all I ever wanted. And I was good at the course work. I got the highest grade in Biology they had ever given. And I have great hands."

I can attest to that.

"Then, one day, my dad didn't come home. He just disappeared. I tried to ignore it, but my mom kept calling. She was starving. She was going to be evicted. She was sick. She was good at sounding desperate. Better than anything else."

"So, you quit school."

"Yeah, I did. I came home and went to work. My older brothers were both working. But they had figured Mom out. They stayed as far away as they could. They knew Mom wanted someone to take care of her and that she would suck every ounce of juice out of their lives if they let her."

"Were they right?"

"Yes. I remember reading a phrase once about a place where 'hope goes to die.' That was my house. I stuck it out for eighteen months. Mom was never well. I don't think she could be well. She wanted to work, but somehow she never did."

"And you were the only thing saving her and she was so grateful."

"No, that's the funny thing. She wasn't. She worshipped my brothers. If they sent a card, they were so thoughtful. I was her daughter. She expected it of me. I couldn't take it. So, I just left."

"What happened?"

She looked up into my face. "To me, or to my mother?"

"Start with you. I never met your mother." I let my hand rest on her back. I could feel her shallow breathing.

"I tried to go back to school. My scholarship had lapsed. When I reapplied, they told me I didn't qualify. I couldn't concentrate. I lasted two months. I gave up."

I sighed and put my arms around her and pulled her close to me.

"That's when I came to Los Angeles and got a job as a book keeper."

"The best thing that ever happened to me."

She gave me a wistful smile and brushed my cheek with her hand.

"What happened to your mother?"

"I didn't call her. Or write. I was angry and, at the same time, I was sad. I didn't know what to say, or how. I blamed her. I pitied her. I loved her. Then she died, damn her."

"How long was that before we met?"

"About a month."

"Did it have anything to do with why you chose me?"

"God, Jimmy, no. I chose you because you were a man."

She actually chuckled.

"Thank you."

"For what?"

"For telling me. I know it was hard." I did because the moonlight showed her eyes glistening with tears. I wiped one away.

"So, what do we do now?"

"It's probably too late to be a doctor," she said.

"But it's not too late to go back to school and finish your degree."

"Maybe. Or maybe I can do what Clyde did and become a lawyer."

Do you have any idea how it feels to be demoted in one moment from being the second best lawyer in San Buenasara to being the third best. But I sucked it up.

"Sure, you'd be a great one."

"Or maybe I could run for City Council."

"You could do both."

"You'd be okay with that?"

"I'd be okay with that."

I meant it, bless me.

Chapter 9

"Yes, massah. They done offered me a job." Clyde talked in dialect when he wanted to be funny, but I knew he was anxious. Actually, I was anxious too. "They say it be good for my futua."

We were sitting in my office, side by side in front of my desk, looking out on the marina. The ocean was flashing and small boats bobbed to the beat of the waves. I wanted Clyde to think I was paying attention, so I didn't have my binoculars around my neck.

Bruno jumped off my lap and jumped onto Clyde's. Everyone has a vote around here. You would think it was a damned democracy.

Karen had told me yesterday about Campion & Gilbert, the big Los Angeles firm that had reached out to Clyde and made him an offer. They had represented Guy Mason against us in his high-profile divorce from Janet. I guess they were impressed with Clyde.

Hey, I was lead counsel. Why hadn't they made me an offer?

"Clyde, that's great. Those big boys are really smart and they do top notch work. You must have really knocked their socks off." I gave Clyde the big, dramatic pause. "It certainly wasn't your good looks and charm. Or your Harvard education."

"No, suh. None of dat. It were my respectful nature. I is a respectful person. I does that whats I is told and I does it with a big smile."

Clyde is a trim, good-looking, well-built black man and well turned out. But he had decked Guy Mason after Guy took a swing at him last year.

He was the son of our maid, when we could afford a one-day-a week maid. That's how we met him. She was a good lady, and sometimes brought him with her when she came in. He would follow Karen around the office and ask questions. Bright kid.

His mother died suddenly when Clyde was about fifteen. We took Clyde in to live with us for a few days until we could sort things out. He moved out about a year ago.

Clyde was smart, although, honestly, we didn't know how smart. Or, at least I didn't. He needed something to do after school, so we started letting him help us in the law firm. He was really good.

When he was twenty, we talked him into going to law school at night up in San Luis. He finished first in his class with the best grades they ever recorded.

It sounds magnanimous, and I guess in a sense it was. But it was the best money I ever spent. Clyde is one heck of a lawyer.

Last year I made him a partner. Karen told me I had to because he was doing all the work. I thought that was grossly unfair. What about experience and style.

I did it anyway. I always do what Karen tells me. "Yes, dear" has been a sound response most of the time. Sometimes I say, "Of course, dear."

I even let Clyde pay out his partnership buy-in. He called it his pay cut. That was ungrateful. In truth, I didn't know what we were going to do without him. Probably close up the shop.

"Come on, Clyde. Your Massah routine is cute, but there's something bothering you."

Clyde looked down at his shoes and his face lost its smile. "Jimmy, I'm scared."

"Of course you are."

"What if I'm not good enough? Or they don't like me? Or what if I use the wrong fork?"

"Fork them." Sometimes I amaze myself.

"But really, Jimmy. What if I wiseass one of those uptight partners? And they've got 300 lawyers. I don't know anyone. I never will know everyone. I could meet one of them in a bar and never know we worked together."

I bumped my fist against Clyde's shoulder. "Hey, you're a really good lawyer. And a more or less okay person." I deadpanned that one. "But I think you've got the wrong end of that stick."

Clyde raised an eyebrow. He's almost as good at that as Bruno is. I practice lifting my eyebrow in front of the mirror, but I can't seem to get the hang of it.

"I won't lie to you. I've got mixed emotions, Clyde. But, they'll be lucky to have you. You'll be fine. I don't know of anyone who has adapted to more change than you have. You'll fit in. You dress well. You're well spoken. Hell, they'll make you Managing Partner. I did."

I think Clyde may have blushed, but it was hard to tell.

"How much are they offering you?"

"A hundred and forty to start, plus a bonus."

I gulped. That was more than I made the last two years. Combined. And that was before our practice began to explore deep sea diving.

"Golly, Clyde, that's even more than you make here." That brought a chuckle.

"But look. For that kind of money, they'll own you. They have to. They'll have time records you have to keep and billing goals."

"What be billing goals, Boss?" Clyde was back to dialect.

"Those firms require 2,100 or 2,200 hours of billable time a year. You know, hours that they can actually bill to their clients"

"My, that do sound like a lot."

"They'll work you day and night." I realized that I was starting to lay it on thick. It was all true, but I didn't know how much of it I was doing for me. I didn't want to hurt Clyde.

"Do you think I'll have time to see Sandra?" Clyde had been dating a cute nurse at our doctor's office. We thought the relationship was going well.

"That may be a problem. But, damn, Clyde, it will be interesting. You'll see things you'll never see in San Buenasara. You'll meet people who've only seen San Buenasara through the window of their Maserati. And you'll work on the kind of deals they report in the *Wall Street Journal*."

"Yeah, I thought about all that."

He was stroking Bruno's ears. I thought Bruno was going to purr, which would have been novel.

"Listen, man. I'd bet on you anyplace. It's not about your making it. It's about stimulation and lifestyle. Seeing how good you are. If it were me, I'd do it in a heartbeat."

Boy, do I lie well. I think I had that course in law school.

"What about you and Karen?"

"We'll get by. Both of us want what's best for you. Clyde, this is one of those times we older folk would call a turning point if we could figure out which way to turn. Its's up to you, but I say, 'go for it.'"

"Thanks, Jimmy. Let me think about it. I'll talk to Karen."

Everyone eventually gets the right idea. I had only thought about discussing it with Bruno.

Chapter 10

BRUNO LOVES SAN BUENASARA. And he's quite popular. The mayor is concerned he may decide to go into politics, but I think Bruno is content with having the local dog park named after him.

Our little town has maybe seven thousand people on a good day. It's a funky little place. By funky, I mean run down.

Our business district consists of three blocks of mismatched one-story buildings, anchored on one end by Polly's Adult Toy Store and on the other by The Lilly Pad. After Lilly's, Main Street struggles across a little bridge over San Buenasara Creek and ends at Hemming's Hotel and Marina, our gesture to gentility. The realtors call it "The Pointe" and charge more.

We have a famous oak tree. According to the Chamber of Commerce, the oak tree was planted by Junipero Serra on his way through the village. Everyone else got a mission.

The modern town, if that's the right word, was founded by Spiritualists around the turn of the century. Spiritualism was big then. Arthur Conan Doyle was a believer. I guess more people wanted to talk to their mother.

The Spiritualists divided up the town into 50-feet lots that they sold to true believers. The true believers arrived on a train that ran through the middle of town. It still does, rumbling through twice a day. They built little wooden houses, one of which Karen and I live and work in.

During the 1960s the town changed with the influx of young folks looking for freedom and love. San Buenasara became notorious for its bellbottoms and hot tubs. Free love tended to make the town mellow, along with the smell of weed that wafted over the entire place.

It has calmed down a bit, although there are more than a few old hippies around. We still do weed, but now it's legal.

San Buenasara is a friendly place. We have been spared the developers for the most part, since the debacle at Franklin Farms. But, Bruno for one, thinks we still have to be careful.

He lifted his handsome face to the warmth of the fall sun. Not me, Bruno. He cocked his head to the side and looked at me, his tongue lolling. Then he dismissed me and went over and licked Karen's hand.

We brought Bruno to the beach for his walk almost every day. Bruno loves the beach. It's his job. He is the self-appointed protector of our fair town from the ravages of a menacing ocean.

The boy is fearless. As the waves come in, he charges them, barking furiously until they give up and retreat. Actually, he waddles towards them, but let's not be callous. He is still brave.

And he always wins. Except occasionally when a cowardly wave catches him unaware. But he shakes it off and gets back to business. Karen and I laugh at his antics, but he takes his job quite seriously.

Dachshunds were bred to hunt badgers. And Bruno is as tenacious a hunter as they come. He has classic paddle-shaped front paws. He prides himself on his sleek long red coat with brown accents. I used to have hair too. I know how he feels.

I was at home one Sunday, around three years ago, when Karen came in. "Look! Isn't he adorable?" she said.

I looked. She was holding a little sausage with long hair and big paws. He took one look at me and barked. Our relationship basically hasn't changed. He regards me as an adequate butler.

"He's cute," I said uncertainly.

"Emma's Gracie had puppies. He's purebred. He was so beautiful I couldn't resist. I want to call him Bruno."

"Why?"

"It's a good strong name. I want him to grow up feeling secure."

"Of course you do."

"Can we keep him? Please."

That is a question to which there was only one answer.

I was concerned about my relationship. Karen had never enthused like that over me. It proved to be a wise concern. Bruno took over the house.

Karen and I stood on the beach watching Bruno charge up and down, doing a brilliant job of turning back the tides. He was going to earn his dog food today.

"Jimmy."

"Huh?"

"Do you think we should mate Bruno?"

Last year we had gone through a bad patch when Karen thought we should have Bruno neutered. Neither Bruno nor I liked the idea.

"Why?"

I find that when I'm around Karen I say "why" a lot.

"Well, he's not a puppy anymore and I think he's interested in sex."

"Have you explained about sex to him?"

"No, I thought that was your job."

"Right. I'll put it on my list."

"But, seriously, I think we have to do something."

"What makes you think that?"

"He tried to have sex with a Great Dane the other day. I was afraid she was going to squash him."

Talk about your reach exceeding you grasp.

Chapter 11

WE WERE SITTING ON the deck of our little house. You have to pay extra in San Buenasara not to have a view of the ocean. I can't afford it.

The sun was setting lazily into the bluest ocean. Little fluffy clouds wandered like sheep in the sky. It was sweater weather, but nice.

Karen was sipping a glass of Zager Chardonnay. Bruno was sipping water out of his bowl and eyeing Karen's glass of wine. I was sipping cranberry juice, my penance for sipping other things too often in my former life.

It was peaceful and idyllic. Only one thing was bothering me.

"Now what the hell are we going to do?"

Karen glanced over and gave me her small smile. "About what?"

"Oh," I said with that savoir faire for which I am noted, "Our economic future, our happiness, feeding Bruno."

Bruno cocked his head at the mention of his name. A little breeze tickled Karen's hair. She reached up and smoothed it.

"I don't think there's a problem."

"Well, golly. Clyde is leaving. I may be setting off into the choppy sea of the unknown with Willy. Would you want to be in a boat with Willy? This decision could change our life. What's going to happen to the law firm to which I've dedicated myself? And to my pursuit of the law?"

"Jimmy, you are a hoot," she said, chuckling. Not the precise response I had hoped to engender.

"This is a vector point. We may have to shut down the law firm if Clyde leaves and I take the job at Wee Willy's. I'll waste all the good will I've built up."

"I know, honey." She put her hand over the back of mine. "Don't be afraid. We might be in real financial trouble if Willy hadn't made you that offer."

"My whole life may change. Our whole life may change."

She looked at me with those big green eyes. I gulped.

"I'll still love you."

I looked at her and my heart did a little dance. Thank God for the lack of judgement of beautiful women.

"I know. But what are we going to do?"

"Honey, the practice has been struggling for the last year. We're barely making ends meet."

"But, look at the potential. I mean, just one big case."

"I am. If Clyde leaves and you do take the job, we'll be okay. Maybe we can hire another lawyer or shut it down. We can refer cases to one of our friends and make some money. If Wee Willy's doesn't work out, we can start again. People won't forget you."

Some would, I hoped.

"But what would you do?"

"Get a job. Maybe also go back to school like we talked about."

"Do you think you can get a job?"

"Jimmy, I was offered three jobs last week."

"Oh."

"I know this is difficult, honey, but you have to figure out what you want."

That was a good question. One I'd spent my whole life avoiding. I had been scrambling since I was a kid. I mean I looked good from the outside.

I was the boy cheerleader in high school. We had this nice little house in Van Nuys. Mom taught elementary school. Dad never went to college, but he was a supervisor at the G.M. plant. Solid English-Irish peasant stock.

There were three of us kids. I shared a room with my little brother. Our folks believed in education. All of us went to college. I didn't go, so much as coasted.

Two years at Pierce, our local community college. Then, three years at Cal State Northridge. I studied Poli Sci because it was easy. I was more interested in girls than Political Science.

I graduated in 1996 with a strong "C" average and got a job in marketing with ARCO, the big oil company. I like people.

I hated my boss. One of the company benefits was to pay for an advanced degree. I went to Southwestern Law School at night. I was pretty good at it. Maybe it was more the motivation. I really hated my boss.

After working for the D.A. for a few years, I started my criminal defense firm with my buddy McNulty of light-fingers in the till fame.

But I never felt like I fit in, scuttling through doors before they closed. Putting on a show, but feeling like I was always walking a tightrope.

I wasn't sure I wanted to answer Karen's question. If I did, what if I failed?

Karen interrupted my musing.

"Clyde will be fine. We had a long talk today. He needs to figure out what he wants too. And we both want that for him."

"Yeah, I know."

It was getting cold as the ocean extinguished the sun. The deck was shadowed and the moon was becoming brighter. I was starting to get goosebumps.

"Willy's job would be quite a change for you. It might be fun to decide rather than advise. I think it will make you a better lawyer if you ever want to practice again."

"It is kind of exciting in a scary sort of way."

"And I think you'll do a great job. Maybe we can even add on to the house after we get married."

She sold the deal with that one word.

Chapter 12

IT WAS MY FIRST day at Wee Willy's. Our world headquarters was behind a greenhouse on a side road a mile into the hills behind San Buenasara. A heavy, musky smell dominated the area like a fog. It was apparent to me that new air scrubbers would be high on my agenda. Everybody for a mile around must be high.

Our headquarters was in a large, old, low-ceiling farm structure that had probably been used for storage. Willy had repainted the building an off-white, but the painters had done a lousy job of scraping. Of all things, it had a bright red door. Above the door in brass letters, it said "Wee Willy's."

The inside had been partitioned into a set of offices with a small reception area. The doors were of the cheap hollow-core kind. It had the sound-proofing of a hooker's motel.

It was apparent that everything had been done as inexpensively as possible. The walls were painted the same off-white as the outside. I think it was the same paint. Thank goodness they weren't having a sale on purple. My office had a thrilling view of the left-hand corner of the dirty windows of the greenhouse.

Willy tapped on my open office door and poked his head in, looking around to see how Karen had spent the $1,000 Willy had given us to furnish the office. Karen had made the place clean and shiny and the furniture was Danish modern functional. You can make $1,000 go a long way at IKEA. Quite a step up from my old scarred desk.

As a bonus, Clyde had gotten to move out of the conference room at our law office. His own scarred desk was a step up for him too.

I really wanted Clyde to stay. I really wanted him to leave. You might describe that as mixed emotions. Mixed emotions are when your mother-in-law drives your new Porsche off a cliff.

Karen said he was taking his time. Bruno wasn't having any problems. He would just change laps.

Willy slid his whole self in through the door.

"Karen does great work," he ventured. "Maybe I can hire her."

I gave Willy a rather absent smile. "I'm sure she'd love that Willy, but she has to hold down the fort back at the law firm."

"Can we talk about us?"

"Gee, Willy, I didn't know you cared."

Willy gave me a puzzled look.

"That's why I'm here. Anxious to get started."

"Like I told you, Jimmy. I got too much to do. And I ain't got too much polish. You got'a take over dealing with all the people we got'a deal with who are like you. Uh, you know. Educated. The bankers, the buyers. Government things. That stuff."

"Right,"

"I'm good at production and quality control."

That sounded right.

"And I got a feel for the market."

No doubt through years of hands-on experience.

"But I get really bored at them meetings talking about margins and cost accounting. And I got no feel for forms. I know what looks good and what'll sell, but I don't like them meetings on packaging and ad copy. I just wan'a say 'yes' or 'no.'"

"Got it."

"So, with us expanding like we are, and trying to ramp up production and all, I got my hands full. I figured you can do the rest."

Well, first, I wasn't an accountant. And, beyond selling my soul, I had never done any marketing. I did have a checking account, often overdrawn, so I was okay with banking.

"No problem," I said.

"Glad to have you here. Want a joint?"

"I'll pass, Willy. I think it will be best to stay on my toes these first few days."

That and I was on the wagon. It hadn't taken me long to figure out that dope was as bad for me as booze. I had been sober for years.

I should have told Willy I don't partake. I wonder if that is going to be a problem. After all, the tobacco company executives had to smoke. At least as long as they lived. I could pretend to be high.

"You get settled now. I'll introduce you to all the folks. Then, we'll go to Lilly's for lunch. This'll be great."

Willy drove us to The Lilly Pad in his Ferrari. I have no doubt that my finger impressions on the dash board aren't permanent.

The Lilly Pad has a unique décor. I think Lilly spent years and a lot of hard nights trying to find her prince. She must have kissed a lot of frogs. There were frog murals, frog figurines, even frogs on the cups. The Lilly Pad was painted frog green. But the food was good.

Willy set his watercress and brie on toasted brioche down on his plate. I was having a cheeseburger.

"Jimmy, I got problems."

"Business?"

"Na. Personal mostly. Sometimes I wish I had never gone clean."

"Really?"

"You get a lot more privacy when you do things quietly."

In some areas. Maybe not in others.

"No one counts your money. You don't got'a file tax returns or nothin'. And I got a couple of ex-wives who think I got money now."

"What's up?"

"You wouldn't believe what telephone calls I been gettin'. Askin' for money and things. And I got cousins I never heard of. Let me tell ya. Never get your name in the newspaper."

I had no intention of doing so again.

"Yeah, well, there's some other stuff too. More in your line. There's some guy named Singer. He called me. Says he wants to invest. He wants to come out. I don't think we want any investors. You take care of it."

"We don't need money?"

"I don't think so."

It was great to know we had a firm grip on things.

Chapter 13

THE CALL CAME IN late the next Friday afternoon as I was wrapping up our first weekly employee party. It had featured cocktails and product samples. I wanted to lift morale. Morale was at a new, if temporary, high.

"Mr. Singer, good afternoon. I've been expecting your call. How can I help you?"

"I'm the Managing Director of Singer Capital Advisors in Boston, Mr. Harris." The voice was high-class and mellifluous. Upbeat. I grabbed my wallet. Call me cynical.

"I've heard a lot of good things about Wee Willy's. You're making quite a splash out on the West Coast."

If the splash was that big, I figured Cleveland must be all wet.

"That's nice to hear, Mr. Singer."

"One of my clients, Eclectic Investors, might be interested in making an investment in Wee Willy's."

"I'm not sure we need any investors, Mr. Singer."

"In any case, I'd like to come out and discuss it with you. Maybe look around. Perhaps we can see if we can find something that would be mutually beneficial."

Well, Willy had said they didn't need investors. But there was that uncertainty. And this fellow had approached them. He was willing to come in from Boston. It would help if they did need money. And how could it hurt. You never knew.

"Mr. Singer, I'd be happy to set up a meeting." I made a note to Google Singer and find out who he was. "When did you have in mind?"

"I'd like to come out next Tuesday."

He'd have to get the CFO to bring all the financials up to date. He hadn't even looked at a financial statement. Get the latest reports from production. Maybe a report from the marketing company. There had been disturbing calls the last few days from vendors who were unhappy. That would need looking into.

"I'm not sure we can do it that fast, Mr. Singer. I'm on a tight schedule. And I've got to get together a lot of information."

God knows how long that would take. Willy hadn't been great about the financial folks he'd hired, at least as far as I could tell. They weren't exactly top drawer. The CFO even seemed kind of evasive when Willy had introduced him and I had asked a few questions. But maybe the guy didn't like having to report to someone new.

"Perhaps we can meet Friday," I said.

"Friday morning would be fine. Can you block out half a day?"

"Let me check my schedule." I didn't have a schedule. I hadn't even gotten a calendar.

"Yes, that will be fine. Shall we get an early start. Say nine o'clock?"

"I could be there at seven-thirty."

Was there even such a time in the morning?

"Fine," I said with some reluctance.

"Is that too early for you?"

"No, no. Perfect." I felt noble.

"Before you go Mr. Singer, can I ask how much your clients have available to invest?" I was playing this by ear, but it seemed like the kind of question an astute executive would ask.

"Of course that will depend on the financials and the prospects," Singer said. He sounded perkier for some reason. "We like what we've heard and the information we have been able to access on the company is satisfactory. But any investment has to be based on the facts. We need to learn a lot more about Wee Willy's."

Funny, I thought, so do I.

"But, again, depending, and assuming we can come to an agreement on the value of the company, oh, perhaps a few million dollars. Maybe as much as $6,000,000."

"That's just fine, Mr. Singer." I strained to keep my voice casual. After all, I had options on 10% of the company.

"See you Friday," I said and hung up. Then I picked up the phone again. This was a job for Clyde.

"Send me over the N.D.A.," Clyde said.

"There are no government agencies involved here, Clyde. I thought you knew that."

I didn't see how Clyde thought the NDA or the CIA or the IRS or any of those three letter agencies were involved.

"Very funny, boss. the Non-Disclosure Agreement."

"But if I'm not going to disclose anything, how can he evaluate an investment?"

"It's for him to promise not to disclose what you tell him. We need to protect the company. You did get one, didn't you?"

"No, I'm leaving that to you." For goodness sake, what are lawyers for?

"I assume you got the background information on the investors and confirmed they are accredited."

I'm going to have to get this boy some lessons.

"They're not using credit. They're paying cash."

For some reason, that stopped Clyde. I guess he was marveling at my negotiating skills.

"Jimmy," Clyde started slowly. "Investors have to be accredited under the law so Wee Willy's doesn't have to give them reams and reams of information. It means they can take care of themselves."

"You do that too." I made a note to look up "Accredited Investors."

"I also think," Clyde continued, "we need proof of their capacity to make the investment before we lift up our skirt. Do they have the money?"

I knew about looking under skirts. Although you usually knew what you were looking for, it was always a surprise. While it was often pleasant, sometimes you could get hit upside the head.

Chapter 14

I WAS HOLDING BRUNO on his leash. The scamp was nosing around the painted toes of a millennial in a short skirt and sandals. She giggled. "What a beautiful puppy. Can I pet him?"

"Oh sure," Karen said. "He's a lover." Bruno was proving that by wagging furiously. The young lady was safe as long as she didn't get in the way of that tail.

She bent down at the knees and stroked Bruno's ears and gave them a gentle tug. Bruno almost forgave her for calling him a puppy. Indeed.

The girl looked up at Karen. "Can I help you?"

We were on a shopping trip to one of the new up-scale shops in San Luis. One of the ones that appeal to trendy young women with rich daddies. For a woman who grew up in tee shirts and sneakers, it was an adventure for Karen. But hey, you only get married once. Or twice.

"Maybe. I hope so," Karen said. "I'm looking for a dress I can wear to a wedding. Something I may be able to wear again afterwards."

The sales girl stood up and smiled at Karen.

"Oh, gosh, is your daughter getting married? How great is that?"

Karen gave her a look that turned heroes into stone in the old days. "No, actually, I am."

The girl had the decency to blush. "I'm so sorry. I... I didn't mean to imply you're old. You're very young. It's just that you look so, ah... pretty. I, ah, thought you would have been married a long time." Nice recovery hopping along with one foot in your mouth.

Karen is a forgiving lady. She's goodhearted and good natured. Among many other qualities I will not enumerate. She let the young girl off the hook, after the briefest of pauses.

"Actually, I was married before."

"Cool. I'm glad you found someone. It's great to find someone new who can turn you on." Out of the mouth of babes.

"Nope. Same old guy." Hold on there.

"But..." the girl started.

Karen silenced her with a raised hand.

"Look, maybe you can show me some dresses." Assuming, of course, the young lady could put down her shovel long enough to climb out of the hole she was digging.

Bruno and I were having a grand old time. But we had the sense to be very, very quiet.

"For a mature woman like me." Karen gave the girl a big smile.

The girl smiled back and relaxed.

"Sure." She went over to a rack and pulled out a blue dress with a short skirt with fringe along the bottom.

"Too young," Karen said and they both laughed.

After our third shop and three hours later, Karen had found one possible dress. I thought it great. On the other hand, I always told Karen she never had to wear anything for me.

"That was pretty much a waste," she sighed.

"I thought that last dress was terrific."

"Maybe. I'll come back tomorrow and look at it again. I may have to go down to Los Angeles."

We had stopped at this cute little coffee shop with small iron tables out front behind a white picket fence. Bruno was lolling under the table. Karen ordered a latte and a scone. I ordered expresso.

She had been picking at the scone like, forever. It would be the day after tomorrow before she finished it. I reached over. She hit the back of my hand with her fork.

"Bad boy."

"I just wanted to help."

"You need to keep your boyish figure if you expect me to marry you."

"Of course, dear."

But it wasn't fair. She had given pieces to Bruno. He hadn't offered to share.

Karen has always been organized, and like most organized people, she is never listless. She reached into her purse and extracted a list. It looked really long. I glanced over at it.

Reserve location. Stylist. Makeup. Order food, wine, beer, plates, candles, silverware. And it went on and on. She looked down the list with a frown and gave her head a little impatient shake. I was suddenly afraid she was about to turn on me and say, "Forget it."

"Do we really have to have all that stuff?" I said defensively. "Why don't we just go to Las Vegas and get married in one of those wedding chapels? I can get an Elvis impersonator."

She put her hand on my arm.

"You're clueless, and you have a nutty sense of humor, but I love you." She leaned over and kissed me on the cheek.

I felt a thrill. Then I looked down. Bruno was laying on his back, licking his balls, looking up at me with baleful eyes. I think he was smiling.

Chapter 15

"FRED, I'M HAVING A meeting on Friday with an investment guy from Boston." It was early Monday morning, around 10. The break of dawn. I was holding a cup of coffee, trying to grease the wheels of progress. It requires a lot of greasing on Monday. I can't afford to grind my gears.

Fred Cym was our chief of accounting in an office of one. He was a beanpole with trophy cup ears and a receding hairline. Fred looked about 30 and he blinked a lot.

Not to criticize Willy's judgement, but Fred had spent three years in community college as a culinary arts major. It was a two-year program. Willy said he hired him because he liked his looks. I hoped it wasn't to cook the books.

"I'm going to need a current financial statement and a cash flow." Clyde said I would need them for Singer. "Can you get them by Thursday?"

"What's a cash flow?"

I had no idea. But Fred was supposed to.

"Fred, exactly what do you do around here?" I wasn't getting warm fuzzy feelings.

"Do you mean when cash comes in? When it comes in, I bring it to Willy every day. He makes up a deposit with some of it and I go to the bank. And Willy gives me a list of checks to write. I send them."

He seemed to be quite proud of himself.

"Do we have a payroll service?

"Na. I do it. That's one of my jobs."

"I'd like to see the list of payroll checks."

"We don't write checks. I pay the guys in cash. Most of them don't have bank accounts."

"Then can I see the list of salaries?"

"Willy tells me how much to pay each of them. Sometimes it's more and sometimes it's less. It depends on how much cash we have. Mostly, no one complains."

"But how do you do the payroll tax returns?

"We don't do anything like that."

I really didn't want to ask the next logical question.

"Is that it? What else do you do?"

"I'm responsible for all the calls.

"The calls?"

"I get calls from all the vendors and let them shout at me. I'm good at listening. And, I keep copies of all of the checks we write. I've got a big box."

"Do you know what a financial statement is?"

"Sure, it's a statement of finances. Isn't it?"

Great.

"Fred, did you ever take an accounting course?"

"I signed up for one once. But it was too hard."

I concluded we might have an issue here. I wasn't sure Mr. Singer was going to be impressed with our financial prowess. Maybe Karen could do something. Anything.

"Thanks, Fred." He gave me a big friendly smile. I could tell it was going to be a long day.

In the early afternoon, I was going to have a meeting with Francisco, our man in charge of global production. Since we have only one greenhouse, his span of control is limited. Given the situation, that would be a blessing.

I had hopes for Francisco. My understanding was that he had been one of Willy's key suppliers before Willy went legit.

"Francisco, how long have you been growing pot?"

The sun was already lower in the sky and shifting the shadows in the room. The wind had turned and was bringing in a warm breeze from the east.

Francisco, in his jeans and old shirt, didn't look comfortable. He kept shifting in his chair.

"Since I was like seven, man, before we come here. I help my father. We sold it pretty good."

Francisco Herrera was about my age. Short, with a muscular upper body, he had rich brown skin, his dark hair greying at the temples. The hands he kept laced in his lap were scarred and cracked.

Francisco was always smiling. Well, not now. But always every other time I saw him. His smile showed several broken teeth. I hope we have a dental plan.

"You've known Willy a long time." It was a statement not a question.

I could almost see the suspicion cloud his eyes. It passed over his face to his lips, which twitched.

"You a lawyer, right? I don't want no trouble with the law."

"Well, yes. I am a lawyer. But Willy hired me to help him, so I guess I'm not. I'm recovering. Besides, I wasn't that kind of lawyer." I have no idea what that meant.

Francisco looked confused. I can't say I blame him. He certainly looked unpersuaded.

"I know him for a while," he said, clearly not wanting to answer the question at all.

"Francisco, I know you grew weed for Willy, for at least the last twelve years. No issue."

"Okay."

"I don't know a lot about growing pot."

Actually, I knew nothing about growing pot. Pot was a lot more basic back in the day. Maui Wowi, you know. And harder to come by, unless, of course, you were in college. That much I understood.

"If I'm going to be able to help Willy run this business, I need to know what you do. Nothing more. And I have no intention of interfering." That was the most honest thing I said that day. I'm a city boy and I don't like dirt.

"I get you man. What you want to know?"

Chapter 16

"How do you grow the stuff?"

Francisco looked puzzled. "From seeds."

"Sure." I laughed.

He looked relieved. He reached into his pocket and spread out some seeds on the desk. "Senior Harris."

"Oh, come on Francisco, call me Jimmy. You're more important here than I am."

He ignored that. Actually, I was hoping he would, even if it was true.

"I was looking at the seeds before I come over here. Real nice. All kinds of seeds. These are sativa. There are all kinds of sativa too. Some strong. Some not so."

"Do we buy the seeds?"

"Used to. Now we collect our own. Better and it don't cost so much."

"So, are these strong?"

He pushed two towards me across the desk. "These very strong. Lots of THC in these. Get very high."

He pushed two more over. They were lighter in color.

"These not so strong. More CBD. More chill. I plant some of each and many others so can blend different things."

"Great." I was thinking back on the marketing campaign. It fit in with the branding. Golly, we might even be able to do honest marketing. That would set us apart.

"Once we plant 'em, it take like three months to grow," he continued, getting into his comfort zone. "First, we soak the seeds in water to soften them."

"You grow several crops a year?'

"No, man, we grow all the time. Start plants in richer dirt, then transfer them to other places.

"All inside?"

"Yeah, easier to control. Use a lot of light at the start. Then about even, off and on as the plants start to flower. Lots of water and electric. But that's okay now. Don't have to steal it. Also, inside can do more about smell."

"The smell is pretty bad."

"A lot of bitching about the smell. We got air filters and blowers. Still a lot of smell. Hey, pot smell. Maybe can do better, but that stuff is expensive, Willy says."

"Will we have to buy it?"

"Willy got friends on the City Council. Maybe? Sometime. I don't know."

I made note of that.

"So, you plant the seeds."

"Yeah, then first, we got'a tend them. Take off the big leaves when the flowers start. Helps the flowers. Flower power, you know, man." He smiled at his joke, giving me an even better view of his broken teeth. I reached into my desk for a pad and made a note on dental insurance.

"The plants, they grow with the artificial light and we harvest about thirteen or fourteen weeks."

"How do you know when to harvest?"

"I know, man. That is what I do. Then we dry the plants. All we want is the flowers and the stems."

"There must be problems. I mean other than the smell."

"Oh, sure. It is hard to get help. These kids don't wan'a do no work. And most of them are idiots. And we got'a treat them in a certain way. All them laws. Breaks. Lunch. You know, treat 'em nice.

Some, they want to steal. I can't kill 'em no more."

Ah, the woes of being legal.

"Other than all that?"

"Spraying, man."

"I didn't know we sprayed."

"Not us. The avocado people. They spray twice a year. Insecticide."

"I've seen the planes."

"Bad for our plants."

"Can we stop them?"

"Willy say the City Council talking about new laws."

"But?"

"The avocado growers got a big business around here. They don't like us complaining. Got friends too."

I suspected their friends and ours had pictures of Franklin on them.

"Francisco, thanks for the lesson."

"You want something, man. You know, special stuff, you let me know. I get it for you."

"That's terrific, Francisco. You'll take good care of me if you just keep the pot coming."

I got up and extended my hand. At least someone at Wee Willy's seemed to know what he was doing.

Chapter 17

I HAVE TO ADMIT it. I was finding it hard to be president. Except maybe I could be President of the United States. He probably doesn't have these kinds of problems.

Getting my head around everything that was going on was difficult. People were coming and going. I was trying to follow up with vendors demanding checks. The bank called to say the account was in overdraft. Willy was in and out, and even sometimes here. It had only been a little over a week.

"Jimmy, how's it going? Great operation, ain't it?" Willy said.

I tried asking Willy about money, but he just shrugged.

People wanted to hire more help. People wanted to fire people. My head was spinning. I must have spent two hours on calls of which I have not the least memory except that everyone was hollering.

I had no idea what I was going to do with Mr. Singer. I should have been practicing my song and dance. Instead, I was learning to shuffle. It was all tiring.

The sun was settling down onto the hills. I was falling asleep at my desk. The last cup of coffee I drank was burning a hole in my stomach. I was still trying to absorb everything Francisco had told me. And I still had another meeting. I don't think I ever worked this hard.

Karen had called to give me a pep talk. Clyde had been by to drop off copies of the non-disclosure agreement that he said we needed

Singer to sign. He waited, standing at my desk, for me to read it.

As far as I could tell, if you signed this agreement and even mentioned the name of the company, we could sue you.

"This is pretty scary," I said.

"Right."

"Why would anyone sign it?"

"I copied it from Singer's website."

"Oh."

"Get him to sign two copies."

"Okay."

He rapped his knuckles on the desk and gave me a broad smile. Then he executed a military about face and left.

My late meeting was with our marketing gurus, Fast Forward. Great name. They were pros. They even seemed to know what they were doing. Maybe this wasn't hopeless.

They gave me a presentation on their marketing research. The vintage and reserve pot idea seemed to be a winner. They had held four focus groups, including one for seniors. I had scanned the reports over the weekend.

Three out of four people claimed to be able to tell the difference between the 2017 Reserve and the 2017 Friendly Farms. They split on which was better. One person noted the overtones of honeysuckle in the Reserve. Another remarked on the extraordinary finish on the Friendly Farms. A large majority agreed they were a bargain at the price, which was three times the price of unbranded pot.

This was all sort of interesting since there was no difference between the two types. We were just testing proof of concept. We hadn't started production of any of the reserve. But the results boded well for the future.

Willy had already been contacted by three people who claimed to be experts and who, for a modest price, would rate each vintage. And *Marijuana Today* was angling for an exclusive interview.

I had been approving packaging and ad copy all weekend. I think Karen was impressed by my diligence and hard work. I know

Bruno was. I could tell by his respectful glance.

One thing was pretty clear. I was going to have to sell Singer the future. I had no idea what the present was. This was going to be like basketball with the lights out.

Valerie, my administrative assistant knocked on the door, then opened it. Valerie is a stunning blonde. Five feet, five inches, with almost all the options.

Karen has a veto over my assistants. She chose Valerie. Valerie is really hot. She's also transgender.

"Mr. Harris, there is a man in the lobby." She said it as though it were a novel development.

"Great."

"You don't understand."

Now, that is not unusual, but this was not rocket science.

"Oh?"

"He says he's from the FBI."

I'm sure I didn't blanche. I felt faint, but I concealed it well. I did drop my pen. But I didn't bite my tongue, probably because I couldn't get my mouth closed.

Chapter 18

HE PUSHED THE BUTTON on his computer and the screen died. He felt stiff. Another long day. Kenneth Singer groaned as he got to his feet. Great, he thought. Now I'm a grown up. When I get up, I groan. Even he didn't like the joke. He shook it off.

This Wee Willy's company was weird, at least as far as he could tell. It seemed like it had a handle on the market based upon its press releases which regularly made it into the media. The product introductions looked interesting. Its Dunn and Bradstreet report looked awful.

Management. Now there was a conundrum. A company run by an ex-bookie with a minor criminal record and a small-town lawyer who had been disciplined by the bar. What more could you ask from a management team?

On the plus side, there was a lot of room for improvement with proper capital and appropriate attention. How could they not need capital with the kind of record they had with their vendors?

They were either stupid or incompetent, or both. In any case, there was an opportunity. Perhaps a big one. He'd figure it out. And he'd sell it. He was good at that.

There also might be the opportunity for Board fees and consulting. These start-ups needed professional help. Maybe even professional management. They wouldn't be the first founders to be ousted. This was a puzzle and perhaps a prize. He'd see. One thing was sure. He was smarter than they were.

He sat back down in his leather chair and put his feet up on his desk. He cradled his head in his hands as he leaned back. He let go to massage his temples with his forefingers and close his eyes, thinking.

It was Tuesday night. He had to take the flight to Los Angeles on Thursday and then drive up to that half-assed town. Two days to think through a game plan.

Wait until the bitch learned the IRS had seized his bank account. She had served him this morning with a lawsuit to increase her alimony. It would almost be worth it to see the look on her face. The lights of downtown Boston shined unnoticed over his shoulder.

Well, he thought, how am I going to put lipstick on this pig. He kicked his feet off his desk and reached for his Monte Blanc fountain pen, a gift from his father upon his graduation from Harvard Business School. He pulled a sheet of paper towards him and started to make notes.

The Eclectic investment was $6,000,000. That was $60,000 a year to Singer Capital Advisors. And who knows how much more if this went well. Agnes McKittrick was a sweet old lady, but she wasn't stupid. He had to get this right.

And if he did, with a lot of money to invest, some of his investment banker friends would kiss his ass and refer clients. Mutual backscratching was a fundament of the financial trade. So Wee Willy's was important. Even critical. It looked good. But there would be a lot of other venture capital firms looking to make a promising investment. So timing was critical. He had to get this deal off ground.

What he had to do was go out and assess this company and cut a deal. He was sure they needed money, even if they didn't know it, and they were far from sophisticated. But that had risks.

His backstop was his own ability to step in. He'd make that part of the terms. Easy. His agreement would set goals for revenues, profits and a lot of other things. A bunch of targets for the company which would allow him to exercise the investor's rights. Basically, the right to take over the company.

Singer started to list the goal's he wanted to include in the agreement. He pulled out some papers and checked a couple of other deals in which he had been involved. Then he added a few more items to his list.

No new company ever accomplished well set goals, so he would be in control, whether he took over management, or just controlled it. Wee Willy's would be his.

Pray God they had a chance. Six million should make it viable. He needed to be sure Wee Willy's would survive, at least for a few years so he could sell it.

Singer pursed his lips. He needed a good run here. This could be his big break He wasn't going to screw it up. Whatever it took.

He got up and reached down for his briefcase. Which one to take. The thin ostrich one, he thought. The thinner the briefcase, the more important the man. Give the right subliminal signals.

He walked over to the printer and grabbed the pile of papers and stuffed them in. In truth, the information he had was awful. But they had the product and he had the money.

Chapter 19

A MAN STOOD IN the doorway behind Valerie. He was about five feet, nine inches, with an unremarkable face except for a distinct widow's peak that made him look a little devilish. He had a few extra pounds on a stocky frame. I guessed he was in his late thirties.

His starched white shirt could stand up to an assault by Mr. Clean. In his dark suit and nondescript tie, this guy wouldn't stand out in a crowd of four.

He was the most impressive person I have ever seen. He was holding a badge case open by his right ear. He stepped into the office around Valerie.

"Mr. Harris, I'm Special Agent Anthony Sturgis of the Federal Bureau of Investigation."

"Hi," I said. I'm pretty sure I didn't squeak. My experience with the FBI has not been extensive and what there has been of it was not that great. But I put on my famous Jimmy smile and got up. I stepped to the side of my desk to extend my hand. I had already wiped it on the side of my kakis. It felt moist.

Sturgis shook my hand indifferently, pulled out a chair and sat down like he owned the place. His face was completely still. I retreated behind my desk. I could have crawled under it, but I hate to conduct meetings from there.

"You are a lawyer, are you not, Mr. Harris?"

The last time I looked. I made a mental note to check the state bar report again.

"Yes."

"And you know that producing and selling marijuana is against Federal law."

"But..." I said in my most convincing voice. I was amazed at how much meaning I could capture in a single word. I prefer two, but apparently the limit here was one. My one word might have been more telling if my voice had been firm.

"Relax, Mr. Harris," he said with a smile I had last seen on a passing shark. "We're not coming for you." I swear he said "yet" at the end of that sentence.

"What do you want, Mr. Sturgis?"

It's hard to describe how I asked that question. I would like to think my strong moral position was manifested in the timbre of my tone. He snickered.

"That's Special Agent Sturgis, Mr. Harris. May I assume you do not want any trouble with the FBI. I mean, we are aware of your former bar issues."

Hey, my erstwhile partner McNulty had stolen from our trust account. I was too drunk to notice.

McNulty got disbarred and I got a free rehab program, at which I excelled. That was when Karen and I had our little problem and she left for San Buenasara. I shook my head with renewed enthusiasm.

"Good," he continued. "We would appreciate your cooperation."

Cooperation was my middle name. Incarceration was something different. Elimination was a step too far.

"What do you have in mind?" I was back to squeaking.

"There's been an upsurge in drug use. And these dope-dealing businesses have been infiltrated by people we don't approve of. The legalization of the marijuana trade has created opportunities for these people. We need some inside help in identifying those elements. We think you would be a hit."

He chuckled at his small pun. I joined him, as a good host should, perhaps with a little less enthusiasm. I was aware of the kinds of people to which he was referring. They weren't nice.

"Normally, we wouldn't care. Potheads are the lower end of the gene pool. I'd give them all motorcycles and make helmets optional."

I felt that Mr. Sturgis did not hold liberal views.

"But the head of the House Intelligence Committee is a conservative and is concerned about how the failing of our laws in some states is affecting our war on drugs. So here I am, protecting our country."

"Wow, you sound enthusiastic."

"Look, I'm not crazy about California. I think this whole state is a bowl of breakfast cereal, waiting for some milk."

"Huh?"

"Fruits, flakes and nuts."

I was smart enough to keep my mouth shut although I am really fond of my cereal.

"Mr. Harris, it's great to be able to work with high-caliber individuals such as yourself."

I was familiar with that term. I used it to describe some of my drug-dealing clients. It described how big an asshole a guy was. Special Agent Sturgis was definitely high-caliber.

"We need someone on the inside of this industry to find out what is going on. Strangely enough, neither your great state nor your industry is very trusting."

Imagine.

"And, while you are at it, we would like to know about any breach or illegal use of the postal service in interstate commerce, money laundering and skimming. That's not going to be a problem, is it?"

"Golly, no. I'm sure Joey Two Gun or one of his goons won't mind my asking a few questions. Look, Mr. Sturgis, why would I possibly do this?"

"It's Special Agent Sturgis and let me try to explain why. There are many agencies of the Federal government that might have an interest in you."

Special Agent Sturgis rose to leave about ten minutes later. Him Tonto. Me, really pale face.

"I'm sure we will be talking soon, Mr. Harris. Oh, and Mr. Harris, if I were you, I wouldn't tell anyone about our little discussion. One way or another, that might not work out well for you."

Two things were perfectly clear to me. I wasn't about to tell anyone about our discussion, nor was I about to do anything about it.

Chapter 20

I PUDDLED BACK INTO my chair. Limp would be called a step up. Special Agent Sturgis had made a dent in my day. Somehow, I had the feeling this might not work out well for me.

Valerie buzzed. "Karen's on the phone." I picked up the receiver. "Hey."

"My, we do sound like the harried executive," she said. "I need you to meet me to taste wedding cake."

"Cake? You want me to taste cake?" I may have raised my voice a tad. Not my brightest move. I'm a strong man, but I was having a very bad day. "I've got this investment guy coming in on Friday and no one here can even find the john."

"Hey, buster. You're the one who wants to get married. I never said 'Let them eat cake.'"

"Yeah, I'm sorry. It's just that this place is in bad shape. We need money."

I will not tell her about the FBI. I will not.

"Besides, I just got a visit from the FBI." I don't have any won't power.

"What? Clyde and I will be right over. Don't move."

That wasn't hard.

Clyde and Karen sat in my client chairs. Bruno sat on Karen's lap. I had just finished describing my visit with Special Agent Sturgis.

"Well, I think he was right about not telling anyone," Karen said.

"I told you."

"I mean anyone else. And Wee Willy's isn't doing anything wrong. I mean under California law. Right?"

"As far as I can tell. We have all the licenses for growing and selling. The consumables are made by professionals. We have a licensed natural products company doing the CBD stuff. It all costs a lot of money. I think that's why we're running out of cash."

"So, what leverage does the FBI have?" Clyde asked.

I thought about that. "Well, none under the law. Or at least, nothing clear under the law. They could prosecute under Federal law for the growing and selling, but that would raise crazy constitutional issues. Although I do wonder how Willy delivers some of his orders to other states."

Clyde leaned back in his chair and crossed his legs. "I don't think you have to worry about that right now. I assume Willy is smart enough not to mail his marijuana through the U.S. Postal Service."

I felt that might be giving Willy too much credit.

"And besides, you just got here. They can't hang that on you."

"I guess."

"So, this Sturgis guy slammed you," Clyde said, "but I don't see what he can really do. I think you should play nice and just forget about it."

"I agree," said Karen.

"He's going to expect me to call."

"He can't expect you to find out anything right away. You can put him off for a month or six weeks."

"But what am I going to do about this guy Singer? He's coming in on Friday. If I mention the FBI, I won't be able to see his back-end through the trail of dust rising behind him."

"Why tell him?" Clyde said.

"I don't want to go to jail for securities fraud."

"Understood. But how is this guy, Sturgis, material to Wee Willy's. He wasn't making any accusations against the company. As I see it, it's your personal problem."

Boy, he was right there.

"They're not going to close down an operation that is legal under California law. Everyone knows that marijuana is still illegal under Federal law. I don't see it."

"Maybe." I like to be definitive.

"I think Clyde is right, Jimmy," Karen interjected. She always thinks Clyde is right. "So, what can we do to get you some information by Friday?"

I didn't know what they could get, but it was better than what I had now.

"Oh, and Jimmy," Karen said, "You still have to taste the cake."

A man's got to do what a man's got to do.

"Yes, dear."

I'm not stupid, you know.

Chapter 21

THE PLEASANTRIES WERE OVER and Kenneth Singer was sitting across from me, a cup of black coffee in his hand. It was almost ten o'clock. He looked wrinkled after his long drive. He was two hours late.

"Sorry to make you wait. The fog just blanketed the 101. It was bumper-to-bumper all the way from LAX."

"It must have been a frustrating drive. I'm glad you made it safely."

"Do Californians know how to drive? They crawl around every curve as if it was an obstacle. And they slow down to let people change lanes. That's ridiculous."

I opened my hands up in a gesture of futility. This wasn't how I wanted to start the conversation.

Singer finally seemed to settle down. His lips were pressed into a smile as he sipped at his coffee. Then he just went completely silent and sat there looking at me with that smile on his face. It was unnerving.

"Mr. Singer, let me be honest with you," I said. "We need money. Our costs are outrunning our cash at this point in our growth." I thought I phrased that well.

Singer looked surprised for some reason.

"I appreciate your honesty, Mr. Harris. And your directness. It saves time and the possibility that we might misunderstand each other."

I knew I did the right thing.

"Is your background in finance?"

"No, not really."

"Did you practice corporate law?"

"We did criminal defense. May I ask why?"

"I just want to be sure we understand the concepts we need to discuss."

He cleared his throat and leaned forward.

"You aren't dealing with any other potential investors, are you? You do understand that my clients will not enter into a competitive bidding situation."

What peculiar questions. He must be afraid I'll take advantage of him. It was going to make it harder for me to convince him to do a deal if he was that insecure.

"Mr. Singer, we are only dealing with you. I can assure you of that."

"Thank you."

"We want to come to an agreement."

"That's why I'm here, Mr. Harris. We may want to invest, but we'll need a lot more information. It may take some time."

I shifted uncomfortably in my chair. I rearranged my face.

"Sure, I understand that. Thank you for signing the non-disclosure agreement so quickly. What will you need? I have revised projections here."

I passed over a single sheet of paper to Singer.

Singer glanced at it. He stifled a laugh.

"Mr. Harris, these projections are for twelve months. And there are no assumptions or backup."

Well, I knew that. Karen and I had made them up last night.

"I'll need five-year projections from your outside accountants with the assumptions that underlie them. We'd like a best-case-worst-case presentation."

That would be easy except that Wee Willy's didn't have outside accountants. It didn't have any accountants at all as far as I could tell. I clamped my jaw shut. How was I supposed to know what was going to happen in five years? I wasn't sure what was going to happen this week.

Singer continued.

"We'll, of course, need to have financial statements from the date of inception, including a current balance sheet so we can understand your asset base. We know that it won't be certified, so don't worry."

Oh, great.

"And, I'll also need your estimate of a pre-money valuation of the company so we can consider making an offer. We can then start our due diligence. We have a team of lawyers and accountants who can come in and do it efficiently. They won't disrupt the business. We do this all the time."

My heart sank. I'd never heard of half of the stuff Singer was talking about. I certainly didn't know how to get it any time soon. And I had to make payroll at the end of the week.

Karen and Clyde had worked for three days. Money was even tighter than I thought. There wasn't enough to pay anyone. No wonder the vendors were screaming. I was darn sure I was going to write my own check first.

"Mr. Singer, I know you need more information, but is there any way you could advance the company some money while you're looking?"

Singer's eyebrows rose for an instant. He opened his mouth to say something. Then he closed it and his face went blank. I couldn't tell what he was thinking. Was my request so unusual?

"Mr. Harris," he finally said, "that is difficult. I'll have to think it over. How much will you need for six months?"

I had no idea. "A million dollars," popped out.

"That kind of money will be expensive." Singer seemed to be restraining himself on some level. "And, let me tell you, no one is going to do that without a lot of control. I'm not sure anyone will do it at all."

"Can you make a proposal, Mr. Singer? We're really flexible."

"Will you take me on a tour of the facilities, please. Then show me all the information you have. I'll work on it today. I can have an answer for you tomorrow."

Sometimes the gods smile on you, I thought.

"Do you have the authority to make a deal, Mr. Harris?"

"I'll need to speak with Mr. Witkowski. But I can do that in fifteen minutes."

"Okay, let's look."

———————

At two the next day, Kenneth Singer placed a sheet of paper on my desk. He was still standing. "This is the best I can do." His voice was flat.

I looked down the single sheet.

1. $1,000,000 loan for 6 months secured by all of the assets of the company.

2. 14% interest per annum.

3. Convertible into 25% of the stock of the company, fully diluted.

4. Kenneth Singer to be elected to the board of directors and to have full and unrestricted access to all the books, records and operations of the company during the term.

5. Lender to have the option to acquire an additional 25.1% of the stock of the company for a period of one year from the date of the loan for $5,000,000 or a lesser amount to be based on an appraisal by an outside appraiser to be agreed upon.

"Gosh, that's a lot," I said.

"I told you it would be. It isn't easy to accept this kind of risk."

"Will Willy and I still be in charge?"

"Oh, certainly."

"Let me talk it over with Mr. Witkowski."

"No rush. The offer expires at five this afternoon. Take your time."

He gave me a big smile. I thought there was something almost carnivorous in his eyes, but I must have been imagining it.

Chapter 22

"AND, SO?" KAREN ASKED. She and Bruno had been sitting with Valerie when Singer left.

"Oh, just great." I may not have been completely sincere. "The good news is that I still have a job. The better news is I might even get paid. The bad news is that we may not have a company. I need to have a heart-to-heart talk with Willy."

We hadn't seen Willy in a couple of days. He lived on a secluded farm about twenty minutes inland. His schedule was, shall we say, erratic.

"I'll go with you. Let me see the proposal."

She perused the sheet. Her eyes widened. "Wow."

My thoughts exactly.

When we got to Willy's, we found him under the weather. Well, actually, we found him under the table with his eyes closed. He had been engaged in quality control.

"Willy." I nudged him with my toe. He batted at my foot and muttered something I couldn't make out.

"Come on, Willy, we need to talk to you. We have problems." Willy seemed to be deeply engaged in some inner discussion. His lips moved but nothing came out. I reached under the table and dragged him out by the foot. He seemed to like that. At least he giggled.

I turned to Karen who had been standing there with her arms crossed. "So, what do we do now?"

It's two o'clock in the afternoon. I guess we have to try to sober him up"

"You make the coffee."

We took turns walking Willy, pausing to pour coffee into him. It was slow going. Bruno sat on the couch with his muzzle on his paws, advising silently.

After a half hour, Bruno joined us in walking Willy.

After an hour, I said to Karen, "Well, this isn't working. Do you have any ideas?"

"Let me Google it." Karen's thumbs flew on her cellphone. I think in a hundred years we will all have long thin thumbs and very short fingers.

"Got it. It says here that if he inhales CBD oil it will block the THC from combining with the canneboid receptors, whatever those are." CBD is the non-halucinatory element in pot.

"We make slews of it. Maybe Willy has some here."

Karen took the bedroom. I went through Willy's bathroom. Neither of us found what we wanted to find and way too much of everything else. Damn.

Karen picked up her phone again and scrolled down. "We can put him in the shower. And drinking water helps."

"You stay here, I'll stick him in the shower." I picked Willy up, took him into the bathroom and stuck him in the tub, clothes and all. Then I turned on the shower. Willy smiled as the cold water ran off his face.

I dragged him out and carried him back to the living room. Water dripped copiously in our wake.

Karen held a pitcher. We got a glass of water down him before he clamped his mouth shut. He didn't seem very interested in departing his cheery little dream world. I was becoming desperate.

"Let's try walking him some more."

After another hour and a half, Willy started to show a glimmer of consciousness, which was a good thing because our shoes were squelching on the carpet. I was all wet, a condition to which I did not feel foreign.

At the two-hour mark, Willy said, "Hi, Jimmy. Who's the broad." I assume he was referring to Karen. He had known Karen for five years. Willy was batting .500 which was great in baseball. Not so much in our business.

I looked at my watch. "Honey, in half an hour I have to be back at the office and either lock the doors or accept that offer."

"Let's keep trying."

Ten minutes later Willy was demi-semi-conscious. He at least recognized Karen. Bruno was sitting on his chest licking his face. Willy was waving his hands, trying to brush him aside without much success.

"Willy, we got an offer to loan Wee Willy's a $1,000,000," I said loudly.

"We don't need money, do we?" he slurred out. He seemed puzzled.

"Willy, we don't have any money. We can't make payroll." I was talking like a person speaking to a foreigner who doesn't understand the language. Believe me, speaking louder doesn't help.

"That can't be right. Money comes in every day." He put his lips together and gave me the nod of one who has just made an irrefutable point. His nod hit his chest.

When I had just gotten my law degree, my uncle came to my office. He seemed very agitated. "My accountant just told me I am bankrupt. How can that be?"

Then he said the very words Willy had said. My uncle looked at me incredulously. "Every day," he repeated in a bewildered voice, shaking his head.

On the other hand, Willy was just lying there.

"Willy, take my word for it," I said.

"Okay," he said with a happy lilt, starting to drift off.

I shook his shoulder. "Willy, wake up. This is important. We could lose the company."

"Huh?" he said dreamily.

"Willy, these investors want all kinds of things. They want information, they want controls. They want part of the company."

"You're the president," he said and started to snore.

"Do you think that was 'yes?'" I said to Karen.

"It wasn't 'no,'" she shrugged.

"Okay, leave him the proposal and let's close ourselves a deal. I think that's all we can do."

She laid the sheet of paper with the deal terms on Willy's chest.

Chapter 23

KENNETH SINGER WAS SITTING behind my desk. His hands were folded in front of him. He waited patiently as I entered. His face was as blank as my paycheck.

"It's 5:10 p.m." he said.

I resisted falling to my knees and pleading, "Please, sir, spare the child." Instead, I maintained my dignified silence, although I may have whimpered.

"Did you speak to Mr. Witkowski?"

"Yes."

"And?"

"He'd like to go through with the deal you propose."

More or less. I'm just positive that Willy's second snore was a "yes."

"But he wants to be sure he'll remain CEO."

"Of course. I don't want Mr. Witkowski to be unhappy. Nor do I want you to be."

Why wasn't I reassured?

"This is going to be a difficult time. You and Mr. Witkowski are going to be putting in a lot more hours. My first motion as a member of the board will be to authorize a bonus for both of you upon the exercise of our option. That would be in everyone's best interest."

It never entered my mind that those bonuses would affect profits which would lower the valuation of the company and reduce the exercise price. If I had, I would have admired the move.

Devious. I like that.

"That sounds fair," I said. I felt good that I could improve the deal. Singer's not such a bad guy, I thought, even if he is sitting behind my desk.

Singer reached down and opened his briefcase. He fumbled through some papers, drew some out and placed two copies of the agreement on the desk. "You are authorized to sign?"

"Absolutely," I said.

He pulled a really nifty black fountain pen out of his pocket and uncapped it. "Then sign here and we have a deal," he said, extending the pen to me.

"Can I take you out to dinner?" I asked.

"Oh, I think so, now that the company has the money to pay for it." He said it with a little joke in his voice. "Are there any good places in this town?"

"Sure. Most of our restaurants close for the winter, but I know a great one that doesn't."

———————————

The Lilly Pad always smells of cinnamon buns in the morning, but tonight it was filled with savory beef smells. It was meatloaf special night.

Our booth at Lilly's was the best in the house. It was the one that had not only a view out the front door, but also a partial view of the kitchen. The red vinyl was pristine, except for the one small place that was mended with red tape. You wouldn't notice it unless you looked. And the frog figurines on the edge of the booth were special.

Lilly had brought them back from San Francisco last month. Handmade by some well-known foreign artist, she said. But Lilly's a sucker for frogs. Figurines, not Frenchmen.

I pointed the frogs out to Singer. Some people just don't appreciate art.

It was unusually quiet tonight, which was fine with me. The recession, I suppose. Lilly had turned the lights down and put candles on the table by the little flower vases.

"The meatloaf is terrific," I said to Singer. It really was good. Lilly ground her own beef and made the meatloaf from her mother's recipe.

"I'm a vegetarian," Singer said. "Do they have any wine?"

"Lilly," I called out. "What kind of wine do you have?"

"Red and white. We have a box of each." Mr. Singer didn't seem impressed.

Lilly is a little woman about five feet, three inches, maybe in her mid-fifties. She keeps her age a dark secret. She's eaten a little too much of her own cooking but she's bursting with personality.

She bustled over. No one can bustle like Lilly. She defines bustling.

"Hey, Jimmy. How goes the new job?"

"Great. Lilly, this is our new partner, Mr. Kenneth Singer. Mr. Singer is from the big city. But I told him how good your food is."

"Yes, sir, Mr. Singer. We make everything from scratch. I get fresh fruit and produce every morning. And, you'll like my cooking. I guarantee it." Lilly extended her hand emphatically. "Well, golly, Mr. Singer. Welcome to San Buenasara."

I think Singer was a little taken aback at the intimacy that is part of our little town. People are up close and personal. Judging from the look on his face, I'm not sure he cared for so much up close.

"How very nice," he said.

"What can I get you?"

"Can you tell me what might be good. I'm a vegetarian."

"We just got in some nice squash. And the broccoli is real fresh. How about I make you some spaghetti with diced vegetables and a butter sauce?"

"That would be great." It almost seemed like he didn't mean it.

"Would you like wine?"

"No, I think not." He said it almost before Lilly had completed her sentence. "Water, please. Do you have Perrier?"

Funny, I thought Singer liked wine.

"Sorry, no. Not much call for Perrier here," she said. "But we do have sparkling water." Lilly is on top of all the trends.

"Jimmy?" Lilly said, turning to me.

"I'll have the meatloaf. Extra gravy. Can you do a baked potato?"

"Butter and sour cream?"

"Not tonight, Lilly. Karen has me on a diet."

"Mums the word then." She walked off with a wave.

"Best place in town," I said

Mr. Singer did his best to hide his enthusiasm. I understand these executive types.

Chapter 24

"YOU CAN'T DO THIS. My God, you can't!"

Willy was more agitated than I had ever seen him. Willy is usually such a mellow guy. Now, he seemed downright distraught.

Willy had rushed into my office late the next afternoon, waving the proposal from Singer in front of him. I assume it had taken him that long to wake up. He certainly hadn't shaved. It looked like he was wearing the same clothes we found him in. They were wrinkled as if he had bathed in them.

"I already did," I said. "Look at the bonuses I negotiated."

He stared at the signed agreement I handed him. "Oh, no." He sank into the chair across from my desk and put his face into his hands.

He looked up at me. His eyes were red.

"Jimmy, please. Call the guy and tell him we can't do the deal. Pay him back."

"We don't have the money anymore, Willy. It was transferred into our account yesterday. I paid the payroll and we've spent all morning wire-transferring money to vendors who were threatening to drop us. I'm glad I asked for $1,000,000. We're going to need more soon."

Willy's face went pale. He raised his hand to his mouth and bit into the side of his finger. I took this as a problem.

"Besides that, you told me it was okay to do the deal," I said in a rather defensive voice.

Well, more or less.

"You said I was president and I told Singer I was authorized to sign."

"You've got'a get out of it." His voice had a quality of desperation.

"Willy, I know the deal is expensive, but we had to do something. We couldn't make payroll."

"You don't understand."

He was shouting. I've never heard Willy shout.

"I'm telling you. You've got'a get out of this deal. Wee Willy's is my company."

Willy's eyes were bulging. I was afraid he was going to collapse.

"Singer is going to sue us," I blurted out.

"Just do what I tell you." His hands were trembling. I mean, it wasn't that bad a deal.

"I'll try," I said with hesitation.

I had to figure something out. There was no way to pay Singer back. And he wasn't only going to sue Wee Willy's, he was going to sue me.

And who was going to pay all the legal fees and God knows, what kind of judgement they would get. All because Willy was second guessing me. Then I remembered my Rule Number Two. If you're caught between a rock and a hard place, squirm like crazy.

I had three choices. I could do nothing. I could write Singer a letter with a copy to Willy and not send it. Or I could write a letter to Singer, send it, then duck.

It wouldn't be exactly ethical to do either of the first two. More importantly, they wouldn't work. Singer and his minions would be out here combing through the company's books and operations. That might not escape even Willy's attention.

Door three. Almost.

Dear. Mr. Singer,

This letter will serve as notice that due to a misunderstanding, through no fault of Mr. Harris, the proposed transaction between your clients and Wee Willy's was not approved by the shareholders of the company, and is therefore void and ineffective. The company will return all money deposited by you promptly. I am sorry for the inconvenience.

I signed the letter "William Witkowski". I folded it and put it into an envelope and addressed and stamped it. I didn't want to disturb Mr. Singer with a fax.

I thought about hiding under my desk with Bruno, but he gets claustrophobic and suffers from flatulence. I gave the letter to Valerie on my way out.

It seemed like a sick day or maybe a sick week was in order. I turned off my cellphone. I had a feeling that Mr. Singer was going to be displeased.

It took a day and a half for Singer to respond. Damn, I thought the mails were slower than that. What happened to the good old days?

There were several calls on my cellphone, a half dozen on my voicemail in the office and four e-mails. Unfortunately, I was not available to receive any of them.

But Karen and I did listen to the messages and read the e-mails for our post prandial entertainment. Mr. Singer cannot take a joke.

He expressed the fact that he was displeased. Actually, Mr. Singer's language did not reflect the vocabulary one would expect from a person with a first-class education. His mother should wash his mouth out with soap.

He suggested that he would ruin me, ruin us, ruin the company and then he would get serious. We had stolen his money and destroyed his reputation. He was going to notify the police, the IRS and God. And he worked for people in Boston with whom we didn't want to fool around. We really, really didn't.

Bruno was lying at the end of the bed, pretending to be asleep, but I think he was listening. He has to find out sometime that everyone isn't as nice as Karen and I. Well, Karen.

Mr. Singer questioned my integrity. Imagine, and me a lawyer. He questioned my parenthood. He called me names. Bruno must have been shocked, but he's older now.

Karen and I went to taste wedding cakes, although I admit I kept looking over my shoulder for those Bostonians with whom I really, really did not want to fool around.

Karen, bless her heart, stayed pretty busy with her wedding rounds and doing her yoga, while I stayed hunkered down in the house. I was getting the feeling that Mr. Singer didn't like me.

After four days, Mr. Singer went blessedly silent. Maybe he needed the sleep.

I waited another four days and then I figured I'd better go see Willy.

Chapter 25

THE DRIVE INTO THE mountains was amazingly rural. When you live on the coast, you tend to forget how quickly you can get away from people.

The two-lane ran by broad green fields. The farmhouses became shabbier as I went up the hill. A cow occasionally wandered here or there in the light rain. I was enjoying the tick tock of the windshield wipers.

I had been trying to avoid thinking about Wee Willy's. The fact that Singer had gone quiet was a bit unnerving. I had expected him to come storming into our offices, but he hadn't.

I hoped against hope that Willy knew where we could get the money to repay Singer. His attitude surprised me. Willy was pretty basic, but he could understand how desperate we were for cash. At least once I explained it to him. And he had to know that we had a lot of trouble.

Willy wasn't answering my calls. That didn't surprise me. I wasn't answering my phone either. But Willy didn't even have an answering machine. We could only play ostrich so long.

As I approached Willy's, the road became narrower and more rutted. It finally turned to gravel. Then it turned to dirt. Getting in and out during the rainy season must be hit and miss. It was already muddy.

Willy had a rambling old farmhouse. It looked like it had been brown at one time, but it had faded into gray and the paint was peeling. A shutter hung at an odd angle. We wouldn't be doing company parties here.

I ran through the rain for the front door and knocked. Nothing. I waited, then knocked again. I called Willy's name. Maybe he was out back. More likely he was just out cold. I pulled my jacket over my head and briskly made my way around the side.

The yard and the farmland beyond were empty. I called out Willy's name again, more loudly. It would be just my luck that Willy had gone to town. For Willy to go out before noon was unheard of. It occurred to me that he may have packed and left me holding this bag of poop.

That motivated me. I went to the backdoor and thundered on it. Apparently, it hadn't been locked because it swung open.

"Willy, it's me." I shouted again. I pushed at the door and poked my nose into the kitchen. You could eat off the floor. It looked like Willy did.

Shattered dishes were everywhere. The small kitchen table was overturned and chairs were scattered around. One of them had tipped over. The fixture over the table dangled on its wiring. I pushed the doors open gingerly and stepped in.

Willy was lying on the floor, face down in what looked like a pool of blood. I acted with my usual calm manner. I screamed and ran to Willy. I kicked aside the fallen chair, dropped to my knees and shook him.

"Willy, are you okay?" I rolled him over. His eyes were open and there was a look of surprise on his face. A screwdriver was stuck to the hilt in his stomach. I grabbed it and pulled it out.

I took his shoulders and shook him. Nothing. If I could remember where his pulse was, I would have checked it.

Willy was as dead as one of his marijuana roaches. I started to shiver. Then it occurred to me that whoever did this might still be in the house.

I scuttled out the backdoor and ran for my car. I slipped in the mud. I crawled for a moment then got to my feet. I felt like I was moving in slow motion. Thank God I hadn't locked the doors. I was wet and covered in blood and mud. Now, so were my leather seats.

I fumbled with the keys. It took three tries to get the key in. Finally, I got the old Jaguar started and bolted down the driveway, the back end of the car slipping, with mud spewing from the rear tires. I think I handled that as well as possible. I must have driven three miles before I stopped shaking enough to pull over and think.

I had to call the police. I pulled out my phone. It was as dead as Willy.

I was cold, wet and bloody. I was shaking. My penchant for discovering dead bodies had to stop. It was interfering with my digestion.

I had to find a phone. I turned left onto the main road back to San Buenasara, running the stop sign.

I spotted a 7-Eleven on the left. I swerved in. Apparently, the driver coming the other way didn't approve of my turn based upon his hand gestures. But he didn't have my problems.

I screeched to a stop or I would have if it hadn't been so wet. Fortunately, the building was set back from the road.

I probably should have given some thought to how I looked. When I burst inside, the Pakistani store clerk threw up his hands and screamed. "Take the money!"

There was blood all over my hands and on my forehead where I had wiped away the rain. My knees were soaked in it. I was covered in mud. My eyes were wild.

We agreed we should call 911. Perhaps for different reasons.

The police officer was young and blonde. She might have been all of twenty-six. But she was trim, maybe five feet, five inches, with small, delicate hands. I stood with her at the door to Willy's kitchen. It had stopped drizzling and the sun had come out. It was getting warm and muggy.

"It's a crime scene. You can't go in."

Gee, I think I had already been in. I don't think she had ever seen a murder victim before. She was staring and looked a little green.

"I've called this in. They're looking for Chief Carsone. He'll be here soon."

Chief Carsone and I have a history. I had the impression I wasn't on the top of his hit parade list. Maybe it was because I kept discovering dead bodies and dropping them on his doorstep like a golden retriever.

Our Police Chief, Walter Carsone, arrived fifteen minutes later. Chief Carsone epitomizes what a police chief should be if bald, fat and lazy are now the standard. He peeked into the kitchen. Then he looked at me.

"You found Willy?"

"Yes."

"What time?"

"Around nine-thirty this morning."

Carsone had sweat patches under his armpits. His forehead was dotted. He reached into his pocket for his handkerchief and wiped at the sweat.

"Did you touch anything?'

"Nothing except the body and the screwdriver. And maybe some of the furniture."

"You're still a wiseass, aren't you, Harris."

Guilty.

"So, you've got blood all over you. We'll find your fingerprints on the screwdriver. Exactly how do I know you didn't murder him?"

"I'm the one who reported it."

"It would be just like you to run a double bluff. It won't be my call, unfortunately. The Sheriff is going to handle this. It's outside the city limits. Besides, they have the resources. But you are going to be suspect number one."

I disagreed rather strongly. After all, what motive could I possibly have?

"With any luck, I can be at the hanging," he said giving me one of his hard, copper looks.

They don't hang people in California anymore. Do they?

Chapter 26

"...IF YOU ARE ASKING if I was so upset I killed him, I didn't."

So here I was in the Willy's backyard with Sheriff Shirley Patera. I was cold. I was tired. I wanted to go home. Besides, I would have remembered if I had killed Willy. I may have sounded a bit testy.

She didn't take the hint.

"Did you benefit from Mr. Witkowski's death?" she asked.

"No. How could I? Sheriff, am I a suspect here? Should I get a lawyer?"

"Mr. Harris, it is far too early to suspect anyone. I'm only trying to get a picture of the situation. However, if you feel you need a lawyer, by all means, get one. We can suspend this and talk later at the office."

"Sorry. This has been really distressing for me."

"I understand. Do you want to go on?"

"I'd like to get this over with."

"Who will be running Wee Willy's with Mr. Witkowski dead?"

"I suppose I will."

She made notes in small, very precise, handwriting.

"Was there an insurance policy on Mr. Witkowski's life? I understand that's not unusual in companies."

"That's a really good question. I'm not sure. But I'll find out."

Willy may have bought the farm in the true sense of the word. It meant collecting on the old man's insurance and paying off the mortgage to buy the farm. "Is Wee Willy's a good business, Mr. Harris?"

"It has a lot of potential beyond a few short-term issues."

"So, it is worth a lot of money."

"Maybe."

"And you could sell the company?"

"I guess. I have no idea."

This woman seemed a lot smarter than Carsone. I'm not sure that was good. She adjusted herself in her lawn chair to look at me more directly. Her tone became more clipped.

"When I say how well did you know Mr. Witkowski, what I mean, Mr. Harris, is did you socialize, go to each other's homes, have dinner together?"

"No. We weren't friends like that." Who would want to be friends with a lowlife like Willy?

"Did Mr. Witkowski have any children?"

"Not that I know of. And before you ask, Willy was divorced. I know because we handled it. I don't think he had a good experience with marriage."

"Oh, why do you say that?"

"Because he told me several times that if he ever felt like getting married again, he was going to go out and find a woman who hated him and give her a house."

The sheriff almost smiled. I know she wanted to.

"Any other relatives?"

"He didn't have any relatives that I know of. Except he did say he was contacted by some people who said they were his cousins after all the publicity about Wee Willy's success."

"Mr. Harris, where were you yesterday?"

"I was at home."

"You weren't working?"

"No."

Actually, I was hiding.

"Can anyone verify that?"

"Sure, Karen can."

"Your wife?"

"Not exactly."

"What does 'not exactly' mean? She can't exactly verify that you were at home?"

"No, she's not exactly my wife."

"So, she's your girlfriend."

"Not exactly."

She didn't respond to that well. Some people just can't accept precision. After all, she wasn't a lawyer. So, I helped her out.

"She's my ex-wife."

"You're kidding. You're living with your ex-wife?"

"Not exactly. We're getting married."

The sheriff chose to address other matters.

"Forget it. Was Karen with you all day?"

"Sure. Except for when she got her hair cut. And her trip to the grocery store." I thought about it a moment. "And an hour or so downstairs at our law office."

"I thought you didn't have a law firm."

"Not exactly."

Her lips hardened and she turned to stare at me directly.

"Are you trying to be difficult, Mr. Harris. Because I don't appreciate it."

I didn't say 'not exactly,' although I wanted to.

"Can you tell me when you went to bed last night?" Her voice sounded a bit exasperated.

"About eleven o'clock."

"With this Karen?"

"Yes."

"So, you were asleep from eleven at night on?"

I refrained from correcting her. Karen is one hot number.

"What time did get you get up?"

"Around six-thirty in the morning. I was there until I drove up here."

"And your ex-wife, your fiancée... whatever... can she verify that?"

"Well, no. She was gone when I got up."

Her hand dropped to her side. The side where her gun was.

"Is she missing?"

"Gosh, no." I never say 'gosh.' I hurried on. "Pilates. She got home at 8:30 a.m."

"Ah. And you were home until you drove here. By the way, how long a drive is it?"

"Yes, I was home. And it takes about twenty minutes."

Now I can add and subtract with the best of them. There was a hole there.

"I see. So, no one can account for your presence at all during the critical times."

"No, Sheriff, like everyone who is innocent, I don't have an iron-clad alibi."

"Sure, Mr. Harris."

"I was just hanging out."

I simply didn't know how far.

"Let's change the subject, Mr. Harris. Did Mr. Witkowski have any enemies? Anyone who might want to kill him?"

This was more like it.

"Willy? Absolutely not. He was just a harmless little man. We were all surprised he was so successful."

Singer wouldn't kill him over a little misunderstanding, would he? Or the people in Boston we really, really didn't want to cross. That was ridiculous. I hoped.

"So, no one had a motive?"

"Not that I know of."

"Getting his money would be a motive."

"Sure."

"You don't know who that might be?"

I shook my head. I was lost. The Sheriff reached into the brief-case that was laying by her foot. She pulled out a sheet of paper in a plastic folder.

"We found this in Mr. Witkowski's bedroom." She passed it to me.

I took one look and swallowed hard. The paper was a single sheet, handwritten and dated six days ago.

It said, "I leave everything to Jimmy Harris. He's the only friend I have." It was signed William Witkowski.

"Now, Mr. Harris, why would Mr. Witkowski make a will six days ago and name you as his sole beneficiary. You hardly knew him, right?"

For one of the few times in my life I was flummoxed. I don't even know what flummoxed means. But I was certainly flummoxed.

Chapter 27

Thank you, Mr. Harris," Sheriff Patera said. She closed the pad on which she had been making notes.

Twilight was sinking into darkness and it was getting colder. I slipped on my jacket.

"I appreciate your cooperation. I'm sure we'll have more questions as our investigation unfolds. Please advise us if you intend to travel."

She clearly thought I was a person of interest and I can't say I blamed her. I was pretty sure I didn't kill Willy.

Willy had seemed agitated about the contract with Singer. Could that explain this? Could Singer? How was I going to find out? Something had stopped me from telling the sheriff about Singer. It just didn't feel right. Why?

Lots of questions. No answers. It felt like home. I wiggled my cellphone out of my pocket around the seatbelt. It was still dead.

I called Karen from a payphone. We still have a few working ones in San Buenasara. I think the phone company can't find them.

"Jimmy, are you okay?"

"Kind of. I just finished with the sheriff. It was unbelievable. Willy named me the beneficiary in his will."

"What?"

"Exactly. Can you meet me at the house?"

I had already told Karen about finding the body. One of the nice deputy's had let me use his cellphone while we were waiting for Chief Carsone. I'm pretty sure word was already all over town.

San Buenasara is a small town and Willy was important to the hearts and habits of a substantial portion of its adult population. So, she probably had heard before I called her. But I thought it might be wise to tell her myself. Mama didn't raise no stupid puppies.

"The sheriff thinks I had a motive for killing Willy."

"I'll bring Clyde." That was a surprise.

"How could he have done this to me?"

"Leave you his money?" Clyde said. "I think it's kind of nice."

I glared at him.

"But I didn't even like Willy," I said.

"Well, there really wasn't very much to like about him," Karen observed. "He was dishonest and manipulative." So much for speaking well of the dead.

"Yeah, I guess that's true. I felt sorry for him. But he suckered me into Wee Willy's."

"Let's be honest here, Jimmy. We leaped, we didn't step. We both let our need cloud our judgement."

I do that every night with Karen. I didn't know it was a bad thing.

"To err is human. To forgive divine," our erudite young Clyde intoned, scratching his cheek. Bruno just yawned. He doesn't care for Alexander Pope.

"But the police think I killed Willy for his money. Or because he snookered me into the company. Or both."

"You didn't, did you?" Clyde asked.

"That isn't funny."

"Good. It might have made this more difficult, Boss."

"Why aren't you working in Los Angeles?"

"I'm still thinking. Besides, the partners of Campion & Gilbert keep inviting me out to fancy restaurants for dinner and I like the food."

"I've taught you well, my boy. It won't be the same after you get married to them."

When I realized what I had said, I jerked my head around.

Karen, thank God was laughing.

"Great to have you on board, Clyde. Now, how am I supposed to deal with the police?"

Karen leaned forward. "I don't think you should, Jimmy. At least not right now. What we should do is get you appointed the administrator of Willy's estate."

"That's nuts."

"Um... Maybe not, Jimmy," Clyde said thoughtfully.

He always takes Karen's part. Do you think there's a reason for that?

I wasn't to be dissuaded.

"Have you been smoking Willy's products. We'll be playing right into the hands of the police. Besides, they'll think I'm thumbing my nose at them. Do you really think that will help?" I was definitive and emphatic.

"Can you think of a better way to find out what's going on? Who might have killed Willy? We need to access all of his papers, his phone, his records Do you think there is any other way to get them? And we need to figure out who killed Willy," she said. "We need to find him."

I looked up. Clyde had stood and was applauding Karen.

"Very nice," I said. "But Clyde, are you sure you can do this? I appreciate it. I really do. But we have no idea how long it will take. You can't sacrifice your career."

Well, he could, as far as I was concerned. But it would have been inappropriate to say so, I think. And Karen might have hit me. When we took Clyde under our wing, I taught him everything I knew. After the first hour, it was all up to Karen.

Bruno, sensing his moment, jumped off Karen's lap and waddled over to Clyde to share the spotlight. Clyde leaned down to scratch his ears and Bruno rolled over on his back. And we thought Willy was manipulative.

"Clyde, you really can't," Karen said.

"Don't worry. I want to do this. And I won't let it screw me up. This is important to me."

His attention was still on Bruno, who was now pumping his leg as Clyde scratched his belly. It's hard to be the center of attention with so many hams in the family. Clyde looked up at us.

"I've got to file Letters of Administration and walk them through. Then I've got to figure out how to get Willy's information. Can I get into Willy's house? What was the name of the guy who was so pissed?

"Singer?"

"Yeah, that one. I need to see the agreement and that letter terminating the deal."

"No problem."

"I think we also need to know who Singer's money came from. His people couldn't be pleased with how this all came down. Didn't you say they were from Boston?"

And they really, really didn't like to be crossed.

"But, there's one thing I don't get," Clyde continued. "Why did they go after Willy? You were the one who signed the letter terminating the deal."

I have to say I was a tad abashed.

"I only signed the deal. Willy signed the letter cancelling it." Or he would have if I hadn't forged his name.

"Ah." It just hung there.

Chapter 28

"WHAT DO YOU MEAN Willy is broke?"

"I mean, Willy doesn't have any money."

"I got that, Clyde, but it can't be. Willy drove a Ferrari. He lived on a big farm. Wee Willy's has problems, but I think it's worth a lot."

"Uh huh."

I was being the soul of patience, as well as its arms and legs.

"Damn it, Clyde, what are you talking about?"

"Well, the farm is owned by a little company in Nevada called Campboll Water. That company is owned by a company formed in Delaware which is owned by a corporation based in the Isle of Jersey."

"Let's fly to Newark. We can look at the records."

"Not New Jersey, Jimmy. The Isle of Jersey. An island in the North Sea between England and France. A tax haven."

"Oh."

"I can't access the files on the Isle of Jersey. No one but God can."

"So, you can't find out who owns the farm?"

"Nope. But I can't imagine that Willy set up an ownership structure like that. He didn't seem all that smart. My guess is Willy may have bought it, but he didn't buy it."

"Clyde, that is an awful pun." I wish I had thought of it. "But we don't know that Willy didn't own all those companies."

"What would be the point? And there is nothing in any of Willy's papers showing any shareholdings or dividends. There's no correspondence. Nothing."

"Oh."

"And I checked Willy's tax returns. All he shows is his $200,000 salary from Wee Willy's and a lot of expenses. By the way, you better hope you don't get audited. Most of his salary is already garnished by the IRS as a result of his last audit. He could barely pay his rent."

"But what about Wee Willy's?"

"He didn't own it, either. The water company did."

"The same one that owns the farm."

"Yep."

"Can we trace the $500,000 he used to form Wee Willy's?"

"Cash. Not even a check."

"Cash? $500,000 in cash?"

"Probably delivered in the dead of night in a paper bag."

I was starting to get uncomfortable. I mean more uncomfortable. I felt like the inmate standing in front of the electric chair in the Jewish prison. The warden gestures towards it and says, "So, would it kill you to sit down?"

"Let me get this straight. I'm the president of a company owned by people I don't know, who have gone to great lengths to not be known."

"Right."

"And I can't quit."

"No."

"Who deal in large sums of cash."

"Yes."

"Then why was Wee Willy's short of cash? Why didn't these mysterious people put in more money? Why were we in trouble?"

"Maybe Willy didn't tell them."

"Clyde, why in heavens not?"

"That nice Ferrari."

"What about it?"

"Didn't you say he paid for it in cash? No loan. Cash out the door to the tune of around $400,000."

"That's what he said. He was proud of it."

"And?"

What's with the "and" business?

"And what?"

"Where does that take us?"

I stopped to consider it. Then the $400,000 penny dropped. "Willy was skimming."

"That's what I think."

"His shareholders, whoever they are, might not be too happy about that."

"I think you could be right, Boss."

"And there might be a lot of reasons Willy didn't want anyone poking around the company."

"Yep."

"But what if they found out. If whoever it was found out that the company was desperate for money, that might have asked questions. Unpleasant ones."

Clyde nodded. He understood the logical progression of great minds.

"But what about Singer?"

"He is an investment advisor from Boston," Clyde said with confidence.

"I know, Clyde. I gave you his card."

"That was a good clue."

I threw up my hands. "Did you find out anything else, Sherlock?"

"It's elementary, my dear Watson," he intoned in his best English accent. This boy missed his calling. "Would you like to know what Mr. Singer had for breakfast?"

"Very funny. I'd prefer to know what's with Singer's and who his client, this Eclectic Investors, is. Do we have another problem?"

"I don't know no 'we' here."

"Point taken."

"It's early days," Clyde said, "but my take is that Singer was in financial difficulty. IRS issues, overdrafts. But he gave you $1,000,000 without a problem, on short notice."

"You mean that he loaned it to Wee Willy's."

"Mr. Singer might not see it that way. And he may have been under a lot of pressure from his investors."

"You mean those folks in Boston Mr. Singer mentioned that we really didn't want to cross?"

"Them."

"Who are they?"

"Well, there's another small problem. I have no idea. The Caymans."

"Offshore too. Isn't anybody honest?"

"We've got the same problem as before. Not even the FBI would have much luck tracing them," Clyde said with an exasperated sigh.

If Willy had been alive, I would have killed him. But what Clyde said nibbled at my mind.

"Why would Singer go after Willy and not me?"

"Maybe Singer figured you would come across on their deal. Maybe he figured he could reason with you? Or scare you. You're the only one he ever dealt with."

Well, the good news was there were no shortage of people who might want Willy dead. The bad news was I had to stay alive long enough not to die or be led away in handcuffs. The world was suddenly filled with a lot of people I didn't want to meet.

Chapter 29

"SPECIAL AGENT STURGIS?"

"Yeah." His grunt was not friendly.

"Hi. This is Jimmy Harris. You said I should call you if I had anything for the FBI."

"Harris?"

"From Wee Willy's. You came to see me." Actually, you came to terrify me.

"Oh. You. Why are you calling me at eleven-fifteen at night?" he croaked, clearing his throat.

It was actually eight-fifteen, but I hadn't noticed the address on his card. Only his cellphone number written on the back. Besides, I had just finished with Clyde and I was scared out of my socks.

I thought the motto of the FBI was "We never sleep." Or was that the Mounties?

"Gosh, I'm sorry. I thought this was important," I managed. It certainly was to me. "Someone killed Willy."

"Willy?" Sturgis sounded less than engaged.

"The man who founded Wee Willy's. You know, the company you were so concerned about."

"Wait a minute. Have you got me on a speaker phone?"

"Uh..."

"Why have you got me on a speaker phone?" His voice was irate. "Is somebody with you? Who's listening? Are you trying to set me up?"

"No. No... one," I stammered.

Actually, I had him on the speaker phone because I had a large glass full of non-alcoholic beer in both hands and I was trying to hold it still so I could get it to my mouth. It was still a little early not to drink. I put down the beer and picked up the phone. A little of the beer spilled on the table. I wiped at it with my sleeve.

"Okay, this guy Willy got killed. So, who killed him?"

I leaned over to the table and sipped out of the stationary beer glass.

"I don't know," I said after I swallowed.

"And why should the FBI care?"

"I think there could be criminal connections. International criminal connections."

"How is that exactly?"

I explained it to him with all the detail and drama only a lawyer who is scared out of his socks can. I painted mental pictures of bearded, swarthy men, hiding behind shell companies, carrying bags of cash and automatic guns or undermining our democracy and preying on our children. I was doing a lot of praying myself.

"There's not much there, Harris," he said with a dismissive tone in his voice.

I had to agree. That didn't stop me.

"This has organized crime written all over it, Special Agent Sturgis. It could be anyone. Even the Russians." Hey.

Sturgis grunted.

"No one will be able to do anything unless you guys get involved. This is a small town. We have a small-town sheriff. It's just too big."

"Let me think about it."

———————

Sturgis called the next afternoon.

"Okay, Harris. I made a few inquiries. We never heard of that shell company you told us about. And we never heard of Eclectic Investors. Singer has no record and no connection to any organized crime figures."

My stomach dropped. Actually, my anus tightened, but that would be crude.

"But, I'm curious," Sturgis continued. "I'm going to authorize some resources to follow up on this. But Harris..."

I was on the edge of my chair. That's because I was torn between jumping for joy and running like hell.

"Yes."

"You better not be shitting me. If I find out you are, I'm going to pull off your arms and legs and then hurt you to death."

Great. Now I could add Special Agent Sturgis to the list of people who might want me dead.

Chapter 30

I HAVE THE FINELY honed senses of a trained athlete. I detected the surveillance almost immediately.

A black and white police cruiser pulled up behind me at the only stop light in San Buenasara. Sid Jenkins gave me a cheery little wave. I helped him out last year with a little credit thing.

Big people seem to occupy a room. With Sid, it was like the room just threw its arms around him to keep from exploding. When he played defensive left end for the Rams, before he blew out his knee, they couldn't find a poster big enough to include his head. He is actually the sweetest guy in San Buenasara.

Sid got out of his patrol car and ambled up to my window. I buzzed it down.

"Hi, Jimmy."

"Hey, Sid. It's great to see you. What's up?"

"The chief told me to keep an eye on you. Told me you might make a run for it."

"No, Sid, I'd drive."

Sid stood there with a puzzled look on his face. Then it cleared.

"Aw, Jimmy, you're havin' me on. I figured there was no reason to make you scared, me sneakin' around. I figured I'd tell you so you'd promise not to do it."

"I promise, Sid." I made an x mark over my heart.

"Would you mind calling me on my cellphone and let me know

when you're goin' someplace. That way it won't be so hard on me. Sometimes I like to get a cup of coffee and a donut. You know."

"You got it, Sid." I took out my cellphone and opened it up. I asked for his cell number and entered it into my contacts. I held the phone towards him. "I've got you right here on speed-dial."

Well, so much for not being a suspect.

I drove off from the stoplight. Sid did a great job of staying on my tail. There was only one road to Wee Willy's and no turn-offs.

I put my car into my parking space and carefully looked up and down the parking lot before I turned off the engine. I wanted to remain instantly mobile.

I was pretty sure I was safe because Sid pulled into the space next to me. But there was no point in being careless.

The greenhouse seemed to be humming along, but the office seemed eerily quiet. All of my senses were tingling.

I knew how to do this. I watch a lot of television.

I got out of the car and walked quietly to the front door on tiptoes. I stood to the right of it, my back to the wall and reaching across, slowly turned the knob. Then I pushed the door open, withdrawing instantly. The after image on my retina told me the lobby was empty.

I pivoted on my right foot and dived in at a crouch. The door met me halfway, coming back off its stop. It's a heavy door.

I was lying on my back and Sid was shaking me. He could hardly get the words out, he was laughing so hard.

"Jimmy, are you okay? That was the stupidest..."

I opened my eyes. "Shut up, Sid." The blue sky was blotted out by the white teeth in his black face. "Help me up, please. And quit laughing."

Sid reached down and took me by one arm. He hoisted me to my feet, apparently without effort. He was having trouble containing his laughter. It kept bubbling over. I didn't think it was that funny.

I left him and made my way unsteadily through the lobby to my office.

"Mr. Harris, welcome back," Valerie said. She paused looking at me closely. "Are you okay?"

"Just great."

She stared a little uncertainly, then cocked her head to the side and continued.

"That Mr. Singer called eighteen times and requests you call him back immediately." She handed me a sheath of message slips. "Mr. Harris..." she said hesitantly.

"Yes."

"I don't think Mr. Singer is a very nice man."

"Really?"

"He wasn't very nice to me."

"I'm sorry, Valerie. I assure you I will chastise him appropriately when we speak." Right.

"And Mr. Harris, Ms. Michaels called from the bank. She said our account is overdrawn again and to call right away."

I thought I still had around $80,000 from the $1,000,000 I got from Singer. What was going on?

"Thank you, Valerie. Can you please ask Fred Cym to come in."

"Mr. Cym hasn't been in for the last four days, Mr. Harris."

"Is he sick?"

"I think he quit. I saw him leave with a box. He kept looking around like he was nervous."

I went down to Cym's office. It was cleaned out. No books, no records. He even took the petty cash box. I took that as a bad sign.

"Valerie," I called out perhaps a little too loudly. "Where is everybody?"

She hurried down the hall. "I don't know Mr. Harris. It's been like this all week."

"Where is all the mail? The cash receipts?"

"I put everything in your office except for the two boxes." We had walked back to her desk. She seemed upset.

"What two boxes?"

"The UPS deliveries."

Now we get UPS deliveries every day and they don't usually upset anyone. But I responded appropriately.

"Huh?"

"It's the boxes for Mr. Cym." She motioned toward two large boxes stacked behind her desk. "We get one or two a week. I always have to sign for them. Mr. Cym comes out and gets them himself."

"Got that."

"But, with Mr. Cym gone, I got worried. I was afraid it was something important, you know."

"Sure. Good thinking."

"So, I opened the one that came this morning."

"Was it important?"

"It was full of money. There must be thousands and thousands of dollars in there."

Oh, shit. I walked behind Valerie's desk and lifted the flap on the top box. There were bundles of small bills with rubber bands around them. I counted one. All twenties. Five hundred. Then I picked up another one. Tens, this time. Also five hundred. Hundreds of bundles. It was a big box. It must have weighed thirty pounds. I wrestled it into my office and did the same for the second.

This was starting to weigh on me. I hoped maybe Willy had an agent who was collecting for us. Sure he did.

Yes, I knew there were issues here. But what doesn't kill you makes you stronger, my mother always said. I hoped this was going to make me stronger.

I couldn't leave the money there. And there were also several other boxes full of mail.

"Sid," I called out. "Can you give me a hand here?" I sealed the open box with lots of scotch tape.

We loaded everything into the back seat of my Jaguar.

"Going home?" he asked.

"Oh, right, Sid. I said I'd call you, but I got distracted."

"That's okay," he said. "I wanted to tell you. I think your employees are stealing from you."

"I know. The accountant is gone."

"I don't know nothing about him, Jimmy. I was just watching folks walk out of the greenhouse with boxes. A guy spilled one. They looked to me like pot buds. There ain't anyone left in there now."

Perfect. How could things get worse?

Chapter 31

"Massa Jimmy," Clyde said, walking into my office.

"Yes, Clyde," I said with an internal sigh. I was sitting at my desk at Wee Willy's trying to puzzle out the puzzle I was puzzling over. It was a warm day for early October. The windows were open and there was a cooling onshore breeze.

The whole place was quiet. Valerie was out to lunch and it was only her and me left. Clyde usually didn't come to Wee Willy's. And when he started speaking in dialect, I always knew I was in for it.

"What's up?"

"I is here to serve you with these papers I got here," he said, pointing dramatically at a large sheath of papers in his hand.

"Ah, you've joined the Marshall's office." The U.S. Marshall normally serves legal papers.

"No, suh. I comes from Mr. Campion, personal like. He done called and told me what to do." John Campion was the senior partner of the huge law firm that had offered Clyde a job.

"Cut the shit, Clyde."

"Okay, Jimmy. These are summonses for Wee Willy's and for you. Kenneth Singer and Eclectic investments is suing you for $20,000,000."

"Maybe I should just pay Mr. Singer and avoid all the bother."

"And they are moving for an order to freeze all your assets."

"Great."

"Mr. Campion called and told me I was to serve these personally on you and to tell you he was going to roast your ass and watch you eat it."

"My, my. Mr. Campion doesn't seem to have gotten over our little dance in the Janet Mason matter."

"No, I don't believe he has."

"And people say you aren't observant, Clyde."

"And since I accepted their offer this morning, he called this afternoon and told me my first job was to serve you and deliver his message. He also told me to smile." Clyde gave me a toothy grin and handed me the papers.

"Thank you, Clyde. And congratulations. I'm glad you accepted the offer."

I thought it was game of me not to cry.

"You are going to be a great asset to them. And I'll miss you."

"I appreciate that, Jimmy."

"Clyde, quit standing there and sit down."

He did, leaning towards me with his hands on his knees.

"Does Karen know?"

"I told her this morning."

"How did she take it."

"Kind of like you, only better. She's a great lady. You're one lucky guy."

It's hard to feel lucky with a company that's out of capital, out of people and out of luck. But, you know, I did feel lucky.

"Well, tell Mr. Campion that I appreciate his forthrightness and I will sharpen my knife and clean my fork."

"I can't do that, Jimmy."

"Now, hold on, Clyde. I know you're on the other side now, but we can be friends."

"I suppose."

"So, tell him. You won't lose your job."

Clyde leaned back and crossed his legs.

"I can't," he said rubbing at the side of his nose.

"Why not?

"It has to do with geography."

"Okay, you've lost me."

"You know, I was really looking forward to my job."

"Of course."

"And you know, I have a lot of student debt and such, even after all you and Karen paid."

"Sure."

"So, a couple of hundred thousand a year looked pretty good, in addition to being a real lawyer."

"Now wait a minute, Clyde. You were a real lawyer here. More than a real lawyer."

"Uh huh."

I was disappointed that Clyde had not known that all those bad things I'd said to him were intended to make him better. Well, maybe a little of it was so I wouldn't feel worse.

"Clyde, you can't leave like this. You need to realize that, no matter what, we still love you. We always have."

"Yeah, that's why it's a matter of geography."

I raised an eyebrow. My mind quickly analyzed the whole conversation and came to an immediate conclusion.

"I'm lost."

"When Mr. Campion called me, you know, he said 'This is Mr. Campion.' Not John Campion. Not John. Then he told me what to do and how to act. He didn't ask me. He ordered me. He doesn't like you. And things became pretty clear to me."

It was sad to hear Mr. Campion didn't like me.

"So," I said. "Geography?"

"I found out I don't like being ordered around. And I don't like pettiness. And I don't like Mr. Campion. I told him his job should reside in the Northern United States."

"I don't understand."

This was becoming repetitive.

"Neither did Mr. Campion. I told him to stick his job 'uppa U.S.' He didn't take it well."

"Clyde, what did you do?"

"I made a choice. You're stuck with me."

It was all I could do not to fall to my knees, look up to the sky, raise my arms and yell, "Thank you, Jesus."

Instead, I got up, went around my desk and hugged him. Thank God I couldn't see him blush.

Chapter 32

"I DON'T KNOW HOW we're going to get out of this!" I felt overwhelmed.

Karen put her hand over mine. "We'll find a way, Jimmy. Or we'll make one. I know you."

That's what I was afraid of. It still mystified me how this beautiful, intelligent woman had married me. Well, she had divorced me too. But now she had agreed to marry me all over again. I know I'm charming and good-looking and all. But I had to question her judgment here.

We were lying in bed. The window was open. It was still warm. October; what was going on? A breeze stirred the curtains and I gave a little shiver.

Karen was naked under the sheets. The wall light above our bed brought out the splash of freckles across her nose. She had an Eric Asimov novel lying face down, open on her stomach. She had turned towards me. Her forearms made her small, delicate breasts bulge against the sheets.

"Karen, Wee Willy's is out of money; well except for boxes of cash we don't dare touch. The people have stripped the place. I couldn't fill an order if I could find out where they put them. There's not even money to pay my salary."

Karen was listening with her eyes shut. I hoped she hadn't fallen asleep.

"And there are creepy people out there I'm scared of. The police think I murdered Willy. On top of it all, Singer is suing us for $20,000,000. I don't know what's going to happen."

Bruno was lying at the end of our bed, ignoring us. His fur was rising and falling with the sleep of the innocent. His leg was twitching, which gave me pause to wonder how innocent our Bruno was. Do dogs dream? Did Bruno lust in his heart?

"We'll get by," Karen said with her eyes still closed.

"I don't want to get by. I want you to have a great life."

"I do. We do."

"I feel like such a failure."

"Well, okay then."

"Wait, what do you mean by 'okay then?'"

"You're feeling sorry for yourself. If that's what you want, then go ahead. I'm here for you."

"But..."

"So, you think I would put up with a failure all these years. Why, I've given you the best years of my life." Her neck was getting red. I've learned that's a bad sign.

I threw up my hands.

"I surrender. Let's figure out what to do."

"Okay, hot shot? Ideas?"

"I'm stuck. I told you. There are so many things happening, I honestly can't think straight."

"We have to take them one at a time, Jimmy. I know what to do with Wee Willy's. And I think it will also take care of Mr. Singer."

"I'm all ears." Actually, that wasn't true, but I didn't think I could bring my other parts into play just then.

"Bankruptcy."

"Huh?" I like to add to the conversation.

"You know, where a lawyer files a petition with the court and the judge decides what to do with the company. What to do with the assets. How to pay the creditors, in what order and how much."

"Oh, great idea." I held my palm up. "Wee Willy's doesn't even have the money to pay a lawyer. Besides, what's the point. Singer will get all the assets anyway."

"Maybe so. Or maybe not. But one thing is for sure. It will take at least a year. The only assets that Wee Willy's has are its name, its trademarks, brands and marketing. But those are valuable. In a year, they'll be worthless.

"And Wee Willy's doesn't have to pay the lawyer. Mr. Singer will." She let that sink in.

"You know," I finally said, "that's not a bad idea."

"Thank you."

She wiggled back in the bed and leaned against the headboard, holding the sheet over her breasts.

"The only way Singer can hope to get his money back is to preserve those assets. He's really stuck." She nodded to herself, her lips forming a straight line.

She paused to think, and nodded to herself again. Then she continued.

"You know, I'll bet he'll pay us too. If you walk away, he's in real trouble. No one knows anything. How can he get up to speed before there's a lot of bad publicity and damage?"

"You're right," I said. I was getting excited now. "Things are so bad, they're good. He'll want to resolve the bankruptcy immediately, with a minimum of damage to the brand. Maybe even just buy us out. In fact, he'll have to. It's all we have, but it's worth a lot of money."

"And worth a try. For us. Of course, he'd have to forgive your little oversight, forgive the loan to wee Willy's and release you from any liability." She actually smirked.

I was liking this more and more.

"Does Clyde still work for us?"

"Last time I checked."

"I think he has a job to do tomorrow morning. I'll call Singer."

She leaned over and kissed me and I slipped my hand under the covers and put it over one of her small breasts and stroked her nipple with my thumb. She kissed me harder. That's when my cellphone rang.

"This is Special Agent Sturgis."

"I remember you."

I will never understand how the FBI can make a hard-on wither so promptly. Is there a course on withering at Quantico?

"I knew you stayed up late."

Lucky me.

"You remember those names you gave me?"

"Sure."

"Well, one of them was interesting."

"Why?"

"We found the name of one of those shell companies was associated with a deal a few years ago for Las Cinco Flores, one of the big Mexican drug cartels. Someone got careless. I want to sit down with you."

"I'm sorry, Mr. Sturgis..."

"That's Special Agent Sturgis."

"Special Agent Sturgis. We're going to fold Wee Willy's and put it into bankruptcy."

Sturgis spoke loudly and with authority. He bit off every word.

"No, Mr. Harris. You are not. I will see you in the morning. Do absolutely, I mean absolutely, nothing until we speak. Do you understand?"

I didn't.

Chapter 33

"I won't do it!"

Special Agent Sturgis sat across from me, his face absent of expression. His eyes were red and he had small horns sticking up through his hair. His stare could have frozen a snow cone. The silence that followed my heartfelt declaration lasted forever. At least it seemed like it.

"Sure you will," Sturgis said.

His voice was friendly, which scared the hell out of me.

"There's no risk. The FBI will be all over you with protection."

And would be equally efficient in arranging my funeral, no doubt.

"We believe Wee Willy's could be the front for a major money laundering operation."

I knew he was right about that, but I wasn't sharing.

"All the bad guys are looking for a way to launder money now that the casinos are closed down. We think this is happening in several states. If we can pull on this loose thread, we might be able to really hurt them."

Funny. That wasn't who I was worried about.

"You want to use me as bait so these guys will make a move because they think I will screw up Wee Willy's for them."

Now, I want to make it clear that I wasn't scared for myself. I'm as brave as a lion. A small one. But I was concerned for Karen and Bruno. Bruno especially. The little guy can't fend for himself.

"Oh, come on, Mr. Harris. You aren't afraid of some small-time hoods from Los Angeles."

The hell I wasn't.

"But you said they were associated with the Cinco Flores cartel in Mexico."

"Well, to be honest with you, we think so, but we're not sure. That's part of what we want to know. Right now, all we know is that the shell corporation that owns Wee Willy's came up in an investigation of a two-bit street punk. Some guy named Comacho."

That was a major oopsy. Manny Comacho was my erstwhile client. The one whose threats against Karen had hastened our departure to San Buenasara. That was a name I never wanted to hear again, much less a man I wanted to see.

Sturgis continued, totally oblivious of me.

"Comacho doesn't have the contacts to set up a shell corporation, much less the brains to control a large-scale money laundering operation. We think he's just muscle for someone a lot more important. He's been associated with the Cinco Flores cartel."

I agreed with Sturgis. Manny Comacho was just a mean, violent street punk with a lot of ambition. All the more reason I desired to remain separate from Mr. Comacho. I needed to change the subject. Sturgis's insistence and his urgency bothered me. I already knew I didn't want to have any part of this. But I didn't know yet how to get out of it.

"Well, what about those Boston shell companies. Aren't you worried about them?" I said.

"The office there is all over it. They don't need our help. It's a big office. That damn city is something else. It's so corrupted they have 5 guys assigned full time to arresting the mayor. I don't even want to mention the state legislature. Besides, they didn't see any trace of a cartel. The Mafia, no surprise, but not the Mexicans."

Wonderful. Now I had to worry about the Mafia too. I had this image of a traffic jam in the long line waiting to kill me.

"Really, Special Agent Sturgis, I don't want to be involved. I'm worried about my family."

"I didn't think you were married. Your file doesn't mention that. There's nothing about children."

I told him about Karen. I didn't mention Bruno.

"Well, okay. No problem protecting her too."

"Not to put too fine a point on it, in rare cases, the FBI has failed to be completely effective." I thought I put that delicately.

"Mr. Harris, I don't think I've adequately explained this to you. The local police have asked for the assistance of our national laboratory in connection with the death of William Witkowski. An investigation that we understand may concern you. So far, we have resisted those requests."

"Is that a threat?"

"Oh my, of course not, Mr. Harris. It's just that we're very efficient and thorough. And I don't believe we would be helpful to you if we felt you were uncooperative."

"I didn't have anything to do with Willy's death."

"Certainly, Mr. Harris. We understand that. And, I'm sure that in the due course of time that will become evident to the police. We just don't want it to become difficult for you. It wouldn't be good for any of us if they arrested you."

Gee, I think he was threatening me.

"And I forgot to mention our close cooperation with the Internal Revenue Service. I'm sure you know that small businesses are notoriously unobservant of some tax laws and under careful scrutiny, criminal activity is often found. Such as unlawful use of the mails. Or perhaps criminal tax avoidance."

"But I've only been at Wee Willy's for two months."

"And I'm certain that would be considered. Besides, there is always your law firm."

He smiled his bleak smile. I had the impression he was conveying his sympathy and his offer to visit me in prison.

"And there is one other thing, Mr. Harris."

I couldn't wait to hear it.

"There are some unpleasant people out there who might resent your murdering their man and moving in on their business.

Assuming of course, we're right. They, unlike Mr. Singer, probably won't call a lawyer. They tend to be more hands-on."

"What are you talking about?"

"Just thinking out loud. This situation with Mr. Witkowski will inevitably come out one way or another."

I didn't like the use of "another" in that sentence.

"But that's exactly what you're talking about. My taking over their business."

"Yes, but as I see it, it's a question of whether you do it with us, or without us. It might go better with us. At least, we certainly hope so."

I was beginning to see the light, as the song goes. And I didn't like the view. I pulled my ace out of the hole and slapped it face up on the table.

"Special Agent Sturgis. I don't think you understand. This business is completely out of cash. We're being sued for $20,000,000 and there is a motion to freeze our assets. All of our employees have quit. That's why we told you last night our only alternative was to declare bankruptcy."

Sturgis smiled again. I wish he wouldn't do that.

"This is your lucky day, Mr. Harris. I'm from the government and we're here to help you."

Uh oh.

"I am authorized to provide you with capital. We will persuade Mr. Singer that it would be in his best interest not to pursue his lawsuit at this time."

How did he know Singer's name?

"And, I'm quite sure your local authorities will be more than happy to cooperate with us on a matter of national importance. We would not want you to be troubled during your efforts on our behalf."

This wasn't going as well as I had hoped.

"As to your employees, we will provide as many as necessary. Our loyal men and women don't mind getting their hands dirty to protect our great nation."

Special Agent Sturgis was showing himself to be an exemplar of that ideal. He saved the best for last.

"And I will be your new chief financial officer. It will give us a chance to get to know each other well. By the way, Mr. Harris, what is the name of your secretary?"

"Valerie."

"She's one hot number. I liked to get to know her really well too."

"I'm sure Valerie will be thrilled."

I hope she had kept up her karate lessons.

Chapter 34

THE LILLY PAD WAS alive with people. I was glad to see business had picked up. It had turned into Indian summer and Lilly had put tables outside. The chatter and clatter were almost symphonic.

We had the table closet to the edge of the sidewalk. We could almost hear each other. I leaned in.

"I won't do it!" Karen said.

That must run in the family. I remembered using that phrase recently myself.

"Karen, you've got to. I don't trust the FBI. You don't either. I need to know you're safe. Manny Comacho scares me senseless." Not to mention all the other unmentionables.

"Jimmy, why are you doing this? Why didn't you talk to me first?"

That was one of the reasons we were having this conversation in public. I thought I would be safer.

"Because you're stubborn," I said.

"Screw you," Karen said.

"Great idea. But in public, darling?"

"Stop it, Jimmy. I'm serious."

"Okay. Look, Sturgis is right. These people are going to come after us. I have to do this with the FBI. We can't do it alone. I don't think we can walk away. It's gone too far. Willy's death has been in the local papers. Someone is going to notice. What's going to happen when those boxes of money we have don't get to where they were going?"

"I can't leave you alone, Jimmy. Besides, you know we don't have any money of our own."

"We might as well use their money," I said gesturing to the big briefcase I was carrying around. We'd buried the rest of the money in the backyard. We didn't know what else to do with it.

I didn't think the cartel was going to kill me for stealing their money. They weren't those kinds of people. They were going to kill me on general principle.

"I don't like leaving you here. I could help you."

"You could. But I would worry. You could leave Bruno to protect me."

She leaned across and punched me in the arm. "I'm tougher than he is," she said.

"I'm not." I think I said that in jest.

"I don't want to go."

"These guys will do anything. They kill whole families. They're animals."

"You could be killed."

I leaned back and gestured surrender with my open hands.

"I don't see that I have any choice. You know I wish I did. If I'm going to do this, I've got to know you're safe." There was a pleading note in my voice. "I'm going to make this work, but I have to be focused."

My intention was to focus on the underside of my desk, after I pushed it against the wall of my office. But I thought telling Karen might take away from the gravity of my argument.

What I didn't explain to Karen was that for the FBI's plan to work, they had to be unobtrusive. That didn't bode well for their plan, as far as I could see. And they'd probably be really upset if they got the bad guys, but suffered me as collateral damage.

"Please, please, call Mom and take her to Northern California, to a resort somewhere. One of those spa things. We need to get her away too. Honey, do this for me. I want to get married."

"Me too, I guess." Her body slumped and the sides of her mouth turned down.

"I know you're right. But I want you to call me every night. I'll be going crazy."

"Cross my heart and hope to die."

Karen's eyes widened and she shook her head. Hair slid across her face and some strands caught the light.

She muttered, "Idiot."

I have no idea to whom she was referring.

Chapter 35

I WAS SITTING IN my office at Wee Willy's with my new chum, Sturgis. It was a bright morning but I felt like death warmed over. At least I was warmed over.

"Now what, Special Agent Sturgis?"

"Why don't you call me Tony, Harris? We're in business together. Pals, right? Besides, we need to be careful."

It was really pleasant. The sun was shining. There was a cooling breeze. It reminded me of a day at the Hotel at Pebble Beach on a vacation I had taken with my erstwhile partner McNulty and his wife. That was before McNulty started dipping his wick into someone else's candle and his hand into our law firm till. Which got him disbarred.

If I had killed him then, I wouldn't have to be sitting here with Special Agent Sturgis. Besides, I probably could have gotten off with justifiable homicide. We all make mistakes.

Sturgis went to the window and pulled down one of the slats on the venation blinds. He looked out and turned to me.

"Why is there a police car in the parking lot?"

"Oh, that's Sid. He's my tail. The local police you know."

"He's a little obvious, don't you think?"

"Wouldn't know. Hadn't noticed."

Sturgis grunted, picked up the phone and dialed.

"How come you haven't gotten rid of the cop? He paused and

listened for a moment. "It was your job to know."

"Well," I said to my new pal, "since we are talking about the obvious, maybe you shouldn't be wearing a dark suit and tie. We're a little less formal around here. Wouldn't want you to stick out."

"Good idea, Harris. I'll get on that." I was surprised he simply accepted the comment.

Sturgis had seemed unnaturally happy, humming a little to himself and tapping his foot. He normally would have been annoyed that I was polluting his world.

He went back and sat down. He looked up at the ceiling and started humming again. That went on for a while. It was unnerving. Then he stopped humming and looked at me. I wish he had continued humming.

"I wonder when Mr. Comacho or his betters will wonder why they haven't heard from us. I guess we just have to wait."

"Yeah, I got that," I said, "but how do we prepare for his display of curiosity?"

"Beats me."

"Come on Sturgis, cut it out. This is fucking serious."

"My, my, Mr. Harris. We seem to have lost our sense of humor. No need to resort to foul speech."

It's probably against the law to strangle an FBI agent, special or not.

"Okay, here is what I think," he finally said. "Comacho is a thug. His only idea would be to come up here and kill everyone. But he hasn't. Why? Maybe he doesn't know yet? His masters are notorious for their lack of patience. Something else might be up."

I nodded.

"Maybe his masters won't let him. They could be curious or wary. This may be important to them. We hope so."

I couldn't disagree.

"Comacho is our only link to them. We have him under surveillance twenty-four hours a day and we're tapping his phones. We'll know what he's planning." He stopped and smiled. "More or less."

"What do you mean, 'more or less?'"

"Nothing's perfect."

As I opened my mouth, Sturgis held up his hand to stop me. "Just pulling your leg, Harris."

My leg had almost come off in his hand.

"We're pretty sure, when this thing breaks, the cartel will want to kill you. Maybe kidnap and torture you to see what you know. Before they kill you."

Well, that was good news.

"It would be the logical way to proceed. Comacho has been their local muscle. His bosses will be putting a lot of pressure on him. If he doesn't kill you quickly, he'll get frustrated. Or scared. Maybe his bosses don't want to move yet. We don't know."

Sturgis seemed to be enjoying this a lot more than I was.

"So, you'll arrest Comacho?"

"Well, gee, no. How would that help me? I mean us. The FBI. You know, the greater good."

I was worried about the greater bad.

"You know these guys never talk," Sturgis said. "They just serve their time. It's healthier. What we need to do is frustrate Comacho and the cartel. Get them to act. To make a mistake. We need to know who Comacho reports to in Mexico. To expose the organization. The angrier they get, the more they'll blunder around."

"If Comacho kills me, they won't have to blunder around."

"Yes, that would be unfortunate. We're working on Plan B. Just kidding," he said, not quite quickly enough. "We want to move you to our safe house."

"I didn't know the FBI had safe houses. I thought that was a CIA thing."

I do believe Special Agent Sturgis was nonplussed. Maybe only a little.

Sturgis rubbed at the side of his jaw. "We like to call them that. We rented a house for all our people up here. We have room for you. You'll bunk down with one of my guys."

It wouldn't be as much fun as sleeping with Karen. But Karen wasn't here, thank God.

It was going to be a real party with the FBI. We could clean our guns together. If I had a gun. I might even get to share a room with Tony.

"We'll have you under our keep at all times. The local police are cooperating. No one will get near you. Unless, of course, they use a rifle."

"That's comforting."

"We don't think they'll do that. Remember the kidnapping and torture?"

I grimaced. "You really are a bundle of laughs, Tony. And I heard the FBI didn't have a sense of humor."

"We do. But, it's an acquired taste. Look on the bright side. These guys don't go out and practice a lot with their rifles. Even if we're wrong, they might miss."

Chapter 36

"So, what do you want me to do about it?" Sturgis said.

It was a nice day in the neighborhood. There was only a small cloud on the horizon. Unfortunately, that small cloud was the smoke from my house that had burned to the ground last night.

My clothes smelled of smoke. I had ash in my hair. I was not my cheerful self.

"I want you to protect me!"

"You're still here." He said it with some distaste.

"The sons of a bitch burned down my house. That's where we live. All our stuff was there. We work there."

I hadn't even known the house had burned down until Clyde called me at the safe house. It was a total loss. Only the foundation was still standing.

Nothing was left except a three-drawer metal filing cabinet. The heat had peeled off the paint. It was still hot to the touch. I wrapped my shirt around the handle of the uppermost drawer and gave it a mighty tug.

The damn filing cabinet almost fell over on my foot, but the drawer flew open. A pile of ash covered my shoe.

Our Fire Chief, Fred Hutchins, was looking over the remains. Fred was an old friend. Everyone else had gone home. He glanced up at the commotion.

"Lucky we saved the houses on either side of you. It looks like someone doesn't like you much, Jimmy."

Tell me something I don't know.

"This was arson, plain and simple. They used gasoline. It was quick and dirty."

I kicked at the ash. My binoculars lay there, the cracked lenses looking desolate.

"And, again, so?" Sturgis repeated.

"They tried to kill me. They burned my house down while I was supposed to be sleeping there."

"Yeah, they probably thought you were there," Sturgis, the optimist, said. "Anyway, you weren't there. Remember, we moved you."

"But..." I sputtered.

"What am I supposed to do? Have a man watch your house full time. Maybe your car? How about one for each of your shoes. Besides, now we have something we can follow up on. We're getting somewhere." He sounded almost cheery.

"But..."

"You've got insurance, don't you?"

"Yes. But all of our stuff."

"Hey, it's just stuff. Think of this as a Zen moment. You're free of all your material possessions. You'll be a better man."

I might not be a man at all after I tell Karen. I hoped Mr. Sturgis would explain how wonderful this was to her. Then maybe he could explain to his wife why he was talking in such a high, squeaky voice. It's not stuff. It's our stuff.

"This is what we wanted to do. Force them to make a move. I just feel badly that they didn't kidnap you. We might have had more clues."

Great.

"Is Comacho involved?" I asked

"I don't know."

"What do you mean, you don't know?" I suddenly had an awful feeling.

"We lost him."

"Surely your kidding."

"No, I'm not, and don't call me Shirley."

"I didn't call you Shirley." This was taking a weird turn.

"It's from a movie. Lighten up."

I didn't think Sturgis had a sense of humor. I still don't.

"What am I supposed to do now?"

"Play dead."

Chapter 37

IT WAS DARK WHEN I had first arrived at the safe house three days earlier. The safe house was the old Wilkin's Ranch, or what was left of it. Wilkin settled in the valley just off the coast above Arroyo Grande. He could have taken any of the land. It was dirt cheap because this was the end of nowhere.

He chose this valley between two low ridges. I guess he didn't want his cows disturbed by the shifting ocean. He may have been a terrific rancher, but he was a lousy real estate developer.

There was a scattering of vehicles in front of the ranch building. An old blue paneled truck. A dusty Ford pickup and three non-descript cars. I pulled in and left the Jaguar near a tree.

There is dark and there is dark. This was really dark. The stars were bright and deep. More like a sequined cloak than a cluster of galaxies. It felt as if it would press the breath out of me.

Someone told me there are 100 billion stars in our galaxy. And there are ten galaxies in the known universe. I swear I saw them all, crowding the sky like God's own Super Bowl. You can say one thing for the FBI; they may be cheap, but they put on a great show.

Most of the ranch had been sold off. There was about twenty acres of dreary land left, along with the dilapidated ranch house, a barn and a peeling bunk house.

The ranch house was set back far from the narrow lane, hidden in a grove of trees that masked the driveway. There were still wild chickens wandering around in the overgrown yard, making noise as they scratched at the ground. They were tough old birds. No one wanted to eat them. Not even the coyotes.

Starlight didn't reach the ground in the shadow of the trees. The dirt in front of the house had been visited so often by rain and sun that it was rutted and uneven. I had to use my cellphone light to make my way to the door.

It was dusty underfoot. I stomped my shoes on the old boards of the porch before knocking.

A swarthy man had answered. I'd seen him in the greenhouse. I had no idea what his name was. But I recognized the gun he carried in a shoulder holster under his arm.

"What?"

"Sturgis told me I'm supposed to stay here."

He motioned me in with a grunt.

Eleven FBI agents made up our little band of brothers. And sisters, of whom there were three.

Whoever made the room arrangements didn't get my note. I haven't slept with a man since I was in college. And I made every attempt to avoid it then. But they wouldn't let me bunk with one of the women. I got Gregory Watkins. He snored.

Watkins worked in the greenhouse, growing pot. That must have been a novel experience for an FBI agent. As it turns out, he was a natural, which must have been kind of embarrassing. The other agents couldn't resist kidding him.

A strapping black fellow, maybe in his early thirties, Watkins was trim and clean-cut. A nice man in an FBI kind of way. He tolerated his colleagues jokes about pot luck and the pot calling the kettle black pretty well. He did kick some furniture in our room, but it wasn't very good furniture. Even more importantly, he tolerated me and didn't kick anything.

We were now ten days into our little charade. Nothing had happened of note. Except of course my house burning to the ground and me dying. Sturgis had talked to the fire chief who was the only person who knew I was alive. Now, he knew I was dead.

We had a simple, almost monastic, life. Except for the guy who, I'm pretty sure, was getting it on with one of his colleagues. J. Edgar Hoover would not permit me to comment further.

We got up each morning at seven o'clock. Breakfast at the main house. Special Agent Sturgis had hired a cook. I suspected she had worked at the Federal Prison at Lompoc before taking up her current assignment. There was no choice of eggs.

Off to work we went at eight-thirty in the morning. Back at six-thirty in the evening, me hunkered down in the back of a truck if Sturgis had let me go in to the office. There weren't seat belts. I have the bruises to prove it. If I didn't go in, I stayed at the ranch and twiddled my thumbs and other things.

Then, at seven-thirty at night, we had our evening repast. Beer was permitted. Not for me. I had asked for O'Doul's non-alcoholic beer, but no one ever seemed to be able get around to buying it. Although they always nodded politely every time I asked.

The highlight of the day was the television hour. The problem with the highlight of our day was that there was only one television set and eleven armed men and women.

I never got to choose.

Chapter 38

THE HILLS KILLED THE ocean breezes, so our little domain tended towards the toasty, what with global warming. We had the windows open, but the air was still.

It must have been two in the morning and I was still awake. For some reason, I was finding it difficult to sleep. The cicadas were having some kind of orgy.

I had trudged down the hall to the only bathroom and back. It hadn't help. Did Wee Willy's health plan have psychiatric benefits? I would have to check that.

My roommate, Watkins, was snoring peacefully, if loudly. Just a month ago I was worried about getting a new client and whether I could afford breakfast at Lilly's. Karen was talking about law school. Now I was walking around with a permanent crick in my neck from looking back over my shoulder.

Staring at the ceiling wasn't doing much for me. For one reason, I couldn't see it. But it matched my mood. I couldn't see much.

I missed Karen. I was worried about her, even if she had Bruno to protect her. And Mom too, even if she liked Karen better than me.

The whole thing had to be some kind of Guinness record on the application of Murphy's Law. Were Karen and I ever going to be able to have a regular life? It was bad enough to have some L.A. drug thugs pissed off at me. They were like rattlesnakes. If you tripped over one of them, they could kill you, but they didn't hunt you down. They weren't as smart as rattlesnakes, but the analogy still holds up pretty well.

A drug cartel was a different animal. Those guys held grudges. They had the money and the resources to exorcise their grudges. Worse, they had the memory.

How did I go from being a small-town lawyer, although famous, to being the target of a Mexican drug cartel?

And, lest I forget, an FBI tool. I was working hard to be the kind of tool you polished and treasured. A really good nail gun and not the nail. But Special Agent Sturgis struck me as single minded and I was not the thing on his mind.

I'm funny and I try hard. And I'm pretty good at what I do, in a lazy sort of way. That's why I thank God for Clyde every day. Maybe he can figure a way out of this.

In some ways, I'm the luckiest guy alive. I mean dead. I have Karen. I have Bruno. We live in a great place. We have friends.

I don't know how I got into this. And I sure as hell don't know how I'll get us out.

So please, Lord, make Karen safe. And, if you could see your way clear, let me have Karen back, Sturgis gone, and some semblance of our old life. I would be really grateful.

I think that's when I fell asleep. It was bright out when I opened my eyes. Watkins was gone. I guess this was my day at the ranch. He had neatly made his bed, damn him. I hate a good example. I had dropped out of Boy Scouts when I was eleven.

I struggled out of bed. It was another day and I had a death to live.

Chapter 39

"CLYDE, THIS WALKING AROUND dead, to keep from being murdered, is killing me. If they don't get me, I'm going to die from running into something while I'm looking backwards."

We were sitting in my office, well now actually his office, at the law firm. I know, we don't have an office. After the fire, Clyde was using an office at Wee Willy's. But I liked to think of it as our law firm.

It was a bit strange to be in front of the desk. The chair was hard, but the view was better. If there had been a view. The corner of the greenhouse was not especially scintillating at this time of day.

"You've always been oversensitive, Boss."

"Stop calling me 'Boss.' I'm your client. Call me 'sir.'"

Clyde stood up. "Yes, sir," he said saluting crisply.

"I'm dealing here with a bunch of idiots. It's been almost two weeks. I miss Karen and Bruno. Well, Karen mostly. Besides, have you ever tried to live with a bunch of guys who wear stiff white shirts? I'm getting the irresistible urge to start selling Mormon bibles."

"Maybe the bad guys are just biding their time, waiting for the right opportunity to whack someone else."

"I don't think so. They're not paying attention. The boxes full of money keep coming. Two or three a week. Maybe they make so much money they haven't noticed."

"Have you told the FBI about the money?"

"No. I told Valerie I'd deal with the boxes. I didn't want to disturb Special Agent Sturgis with housekeeping details."

"What are you doing with them?"

"I've got most of it buried in the backyard. If something doesn't happen soon, I'm going to have to rent a vacant lot."

"So, tip off the hoods."

"We can't just knock on their door and say, 'Hi, I'm from the FBI. Have you noticed...'"

"Didn't say you should."

"You have an idea?"

"Maybe, but I won't tell you unless you let me call you Boss, sir."

"Come on, Clyde, we're dealing with death or death here."

"I can see that, Boss, sir."

"Good, now tell me your idea."

"Well, as I understand it, the bad guys were supposed to get upset because you muscled in on their business."

"Right."

"So, they tried to kill you.

"Right."

"And they succeeded."

"Well, yes and no."

"So, they think they are okay. They haven't figured out there is someone else involved."

"Apparently not. It's the only reason I can think of that they haven't made a move."

"They probably believe you were smart enough to act alone."

"Wait a minute."

He didn't.

"They own Wee Willy's through those shell companies."

"We think so."

"What if they discovered they didn't?"

"I would catch their attention. Do you think we should sell it?"

"That might work. But it's not very subtle. And it would be difficult to bring it to their attention. But you're getting warm. Good job, sir."

"Don't be an asshole, Clyde. I'm dealing with the FBI and I

have assholes up to my bum. What do you think we should do?"

"Sell stock to the public."

"Great idea, Clyde. What do you mean?" I have a razor-like intellect.

"Look, Jimmy. Start at the beginning. This is a major Mexican drug cartel you're dealing with."

"That's what the FBI says. Thanks for reminding me."

"They make so much money, a few hundred thousand dollars a week can slip through the cracks."

"It looks like it."

"And they own Wee Willy's."

"So far, your logic is flawless, but I'm going to go to sleep unless you get to the point."

"The idea here is that with a lot of money, they have a lot of business interests. It would stand to reason. That means they have a lot of lawyers."

"Sure, for their businesses in the U.S."

"If you owned something, it might upset you if you found out someone else was trying to sell it. It might indicate something is wrong."

"Clyde, this is where we started."

"But, here's the subtle part. We make up documents for an initial public offering. You know, a red herring prospectus. The FBI hires investment bankers."

"Clyde, we can't sell the stock. We'll go to jail."

"We don't sell the stock. We get the prospectus to all the lawyers who might be representing the cartel. Or any cartel for that matter. It takes a pretty sophisticated bunch of lawyers to form corporate shells and deal with taxes and a lot of diverse business interests. I'll bet the FBI has a pretty good idea of the kind of lawyers we're talking about."

"Okay. Granted." I was nodding so much, my head was in danger of falling off.

"And it wouldn't look suspicious. Underwriters do it all the time to promote interest in an offering they're trying to sell.

Someone will notice Wee Willy's. It's not exactly a common name. If one of their lawyers notices and checks, he'll be on the line with his clients in minutes and they'll have a hissy fit."

This boy was an evil genius. I was proud to know him.

"And wait until the lawyer tells his client about underwriter due diligence."

"Explain."

"Underwriters comb through the business and records of any company they take public. They have to in order to avoid fraud claims. I understand these cartels don't like folks poking into their affairs. I suspect they'll be even more pissed. It will put a lot of pressure on the them to do something right away."

"Like kill someone."

"Well, yeah. That could be a downside. But Karen's safe. And you're already dead."

"Clyde, you do have a way with words. How do you know all about this public offering stuff?"

"Mr. Campion suggested I might like to take a course while I was thinking about their offer. On the firm, of course. It interested me. You know, Jimmy, maybe you should think of improving our firm benefits."

"I certainly will, if I can avoid becoming piecework in the meantime." It's good for everyone to be on the same page.

Chapter 40

Something hard hit the wall in Sturgis's office. It sounded like a fist. Sound-proofing in our world headquarters left something to be desired.

"What a bunch of fucking idiots," he shouted, his voice muted by the thin wall.

I could hear his shoes on the tile floor in the hallway. I believe he was on his way to share with me. He barged in without knocking. His face was red.

"Do you have any idea how much it costs a week for the FBI to run this place?"

"No."

"Well, damn it, I was just told precisely how much by my boss. Harris, I really don't like accounting."

And this was my chief financial officer.

"Look, it isn't your fault they haven't tried to kill someone else yet."

"Actually, it is. I sold them this operation. They want results." He looked at me intently. "I may have to kill you again myself." He was kidding, I think.

"They're not paying attention." I had been waiting to share it with Sturgis. This seemed like a good time. "You need to tug on their sleeve."

"Cool it, Harris. I don't need a wise-ass right now."

"No, I've got an idea."

Well, it was almost mine.

"Great. An asshole with an idea."

"Comacho doesn't get it. We need to appeal to a higher authority. You know, like we should hit the cartel between the eyes with a 2x4."

"And how do you intend to do that, smart guy?"

I explained the idea to him. I thought I saw the light of admiration flicker in his eyes.

"We know these cartels have their fingers in a lot of businesses," Sturgis said. "We know they use lawyers, even some big corporate guys."

"You must have found out which law firms formed all those shell companies?"

"I guess. I never looked. We never thought the lawyers were a good way to get at these people. The lawyers may not even know they're representing the cartel. But I like the idea. You've obviously thought this through."

"I have."

At least I listened closely.

"I didn't think you were that bright."

Now that hurt. I was about to save his bacon and put mine in the frying pan again.

"So, it's a good idea. Let's file an initial public offering," Sturgis said. "An IPO. I like that. Kind of like FBI." He said that with some enthusiasm. "And I'll take a look to see if there are any law firms that are involved. What should we do next, genius?"

"We have to prepare a red herring."

"A red herring?"

"It's a preliminary printed prospectus for a public offering. It's called a 'red herring' because the S.E.C. requires it to say 'Preliminary Prospectus' in red ink along the edge. The prospectus tells all the facts about the company so an investor can make an evaluation."

"There's nothing here. This company is nonexistent."

"All the better. We'll make up all the numbers and the business stuff. I can get Clyde to do it."

"Who's Clyde?"

"He's my law partner."

"Okay. Let's get going."

I held up my hand, palm out, to pause Special Agent Sturgis in his assent. "Of course, you'll have to pay Clyde."

He frowned. "What do you mean?"

"You know. Legal fees."

"Surely, you jest."

"No. And don't call me Shirley." I had looked up the movie.

He ignored me. "How much?"

"Four hundred twenty-five dollars an hour."

"That's outrageous."

"Yep."

Actually, it was twice Clyde's hourly rate. But the law firm deserved it. We needed the money for firm benefits.

"I won't do it."

"Okay." I learned that one from Karen.

"What do you mean, okay?"

"Get someone else. You'll need a lawyer. It's a complex form and requires a great deal of expertise if it's going to fool another lawyer. I know it will take twice as long. And, probably cost twice as much. But I can understand your position."

"Shit."

"It's your choice Special Agent Sturgis... I mean, Tony."

Sturgis went quiet, which might have been better if he wasn't staring at me murderously.

"I'm going to do this, Harris. But, Harris..."

I cocked my head in anticipation.

"I'm going to stick this up your ass."

I just hoped my ass was attached to the rest of me when he tried.

Chapter 41

IT WAS ALMOST FOUR in the morning. I was sleeping on the rug in my office at Wee Willy's with my arms around a pizza box. It wasn't as good as Karen. But it was there.

Two pieces of cold pepperoni pizza were left inside. Grease darkened the corners of the box.

I love cold pizza. So does Bruno, but he wasn't here. His loss.

All the lights were on. My eyes popped open. I had heard a sound that made my blood run cold. Special Agent Sturgis was laughing. I mean really laughing.

"You know, this is kind of fun," he said to Clyde. He never said that to me. "How much profit do you think Wee Willy's should make for last year?"

"Whatever you want, Tony," Clyde said in a jocular voice, "Just don't make it too high. We need this to be believable."

'Tony?' Clyde called him Tony? Clyde was sitting at his computer, his fingers darting across the keyboard. The printer clicked out pages in the background.

"Yeah, I guess so. I just want Wee Willy's to be successful," Sturgis said.

"You mean, seem successful," Clyde corrected.

"I guess."

"You've done a great job on the product descriptions and the financials, Tony."

"I never knew being a lawyer could be this much fun. I should have finished law school.

"You went to law school?" Clyde asked.

"St. John's. Quit after a year. You?"

"I went to a local school up in San Luis Obispo. Went at night." Clyde didn't tell him he had done it while working full time for us as a paralegal and finished first in his class. Or that his paper on tax emoluments had been published in the Stanford Law Review.

"Do you like working up here?"

"Yeah, I was offered a job in L.A., but I turned it down."

"Who with?

"Campion & Gilbert."

Sturgis whistled.

"Good morning," I said brightly. I stood up and stretched. The clicking of my vertebrae did a catchy little rumba.

"Sorry I pooped out on you," I said through a yawn. "Old age, I guess. How's it coming?"

"Harris, this partner of yours is a genius." He gave Clyde a playful bump on the shoulder. "I don't know why he's working for you in this shithole. It would be a one-horse town if they had a horse."

I did not inform Special Agent Sturgis that we had several horses, as well as many chickens. But I intended to inform the Chamber of Commerce who would undoubtedly boycott the FBI forthwith.

I stretched again. It felt good. My floor is hard, but I'm harder.

We had been working day and night for two days. There must have been two inches of paper stacked on the desk.

"When do you think we'll have a first draft, Clyde?" I asked.

"Maybe tomorrow."

"You must be exhausted."

"I'm good."

"Should I go to The Lilly Pad and bring something back?" We warriors get hungry. I was.

"Jimmy, it's four in the morning."

"Right."

"Besides, you need to start reading the draft while Tony and I work on the appendices."

"You want me to put my hand to the forepart and massage it?" Clyde groaned.

"I knew I should have shot him," Sturgis said.

I thought that had been a rather witty remark. Perhaps they had been up too long.

I wandered over to the pizza box and grabbed a slice of cold pizza. Clyde looked at me and shook his head in disgust. I ignored him and took a large bite. It was great.

Then I sat down at the desk and pulled the pile of paper towards me. The grease on my fingers stained the pages. I checked to make sure Clyde wasn't looking.

I settled down to read. It looked pretty convincing to me. But what did I know?

"Harris, we need to get this out by tomorrow night." Sturgis said, getting up to flex his shoulders. "The Bureau has hired Parker & Simenon to handle the deal."

"How did you get them?"

Even I knew of Parker & Simenon. They were a boutique investment banking firm that had made a name for themselves in the Silicon Valley during the 1980s. They would be believable.

"They owe us."

"Do they know the deal's a phony?"

"They know everything they need to know. They'll have a banker here on Wednesday," Sturgis said. That gave us four days.

"Jimmy, we plan to go to the printers on Sunday and have red herrings by Monday. That will give us Tuesday to fix anything."

"Any idea how many copies we'll need?" I asked.

Sturgis answered.

"My guys went through all the shell companies and every incorporation document. We cross referenced our files on all the cartels. There are probably a few dozen firms. And maybe another 20 more we want to cover. We don't need to be shy. Maybe 200 copies. We'll send the red herring out in the mail. Then the bankers will follow up with a call. That should get someone's attention."

I finally felt like we were doing something. But it was kind of like the girl in the limerick who climbed on the back of the tiger. It didn't work out so well for the girl, as I recall.

Chapter 42

WE DIDN'T HAVE LONG to wait for a response. It was only a week, most of which I spent huddling in the corner of my office. The response wasn't what we expected. A Fed-Ex envelope was delivered.

Sturgis suggested I open it. I demurred. He grudgingly took the thin package from me and gingerly pulled the tab. It wasn't a bomb, at least of the classic kind.

"Well, I'll be damned," he said. I was pretty sure he was going to get his wish. He handed me the three sheets of paper with Campion & Gilbert's name engraved on the top of thick bond paper. The cover letter was signed by John Campion.

It was a letter of intent to buy Wee Willy's for $27,000,000. That was about twenty percent more than the valuation in our make-believe prospectus, which was interesting. The proposed purchaser was XYZ Acquisition Company, so that told us nothing. It looked like Mr. Campion was both trying to put us out of business by suing us for $20,000,000 and trying to buy us.

Campion's letter requested that we present the purchase offer to the board. It was conditioned on suspending our public offering immediately.

Clyde was sitting in the corner reading the *San Buenasara Beacon*. He folded up the paper and looked at us. "They're buying time, not us," he said.

"Huh?" I reposted.

"Sure. We hit the mule between the eyes with the 2x4. We've got its attention. Now its standing still, trying to figure out what to do. This offer freezes the underwriter's due diligence while they determine what we want. Or if they should kill us. It's really quite bright. I bet Campion suggested it."

"But how do you think he's managing to represent Singer in the lawsuit and this buyer? There must be a little conflict."

"That is one of the interesting questions. It suggests that this client is important to them," Clyde observed. "Besides, he probably promised Singer his money if the deal went through."

Sturgis was just listening. But he was listening intently.

"Explain what you mean, Clyde," he said.

"Look, Tony, they know, or at least their lawyers know, that we can't go ahead with the public offering without presenting this offer to the board. I suspect they made it a really good offer for that reason. They want to freeze us in place."

"Why does it freeze us in place?'

"They figure it will take a week or so for our underwriters to analyze the terms of the offer and prepare a report and maybe another week for the board to consider the offer and reach a decision. And that gives them time to find out who's involved and what is going on. We pretty well blindsided them. With Jimmy dead, they thought they were out of the woods."

Sturgis looked adrift. He hadn't expected anything this subtle. All of his guys had oiled their guns when we sent out the red herring.

"Who's on the board?" he asked.

"I don't know," I said.

"Who are the stockholders?"

"There are all these shell companies. Willy, I suppose, but he's dead. Dead shareholders can't vote."

"But you're the administrator of Willy's estate," Clyde said. "You can."

"No, I can't. I'm dead."

"No, you're not," said Clyde. "You're only dead publicly. Not for our purposes."

That was good to know.

"So, it works legally?"

"Not that it matters. But who's going to object?"

That was a good question. The FBI would certainly be interested in anyone who came forward.

"No one," Sturgis said.

"Well, then," Clyde said, rubbing his hands together, "we have a clean slate. They want time. Let's press 'em."

We worked all morning on a response to the purchase offer. It had to sound just right to avoid raising any red flags.

I read the letter to Sturgis before he signed it.

Gentlemen,

Thank you for your proposed Letter of Intent. Our board has met in emergency session. Unfortunately, Wee Willy's cannot consider your offer under the present circumstances. While what you propose seems fair, you have presented no proof of financial capability. Until presented with such proof in the form of a letter of credit, bank records or similar information, the board is unable act on your offer. Until such time, the company will proceed with its public offering.

"That sounds okay," Sturgis said. Clyde nodded. He signed the letter in his capacity as chief financial officer. I addressed a Fed-Ex envelope to my old buddy John Campion and slipped the letter in.

"Well, this is getting interesting," Sturgis said. "If they give us the financial information, we can walk it back. If not, they're going to have to come after us."

He didn't mean us.

"Great strategy, Clyde. The ball's in their court. I think I better make a few calls," Sturgis said.

Chapter 43

I CAME IN EARLY in the morning. I hadn't been murdered in my sleep, no thanks to the FBI. Sturgis made me lay on the floor in the back of his car on our way into the office. He kept yelling, "Play dead, boy. Good boy."

Our underwriter, Willis Jeffries, was on his way up from Los Angeles to plan the dog and pony show to follow up the calls to the lawyers who had received the red herring. I went into my office to try to take a nap.

No luck. It sounded like a bear was thumping at the base of my office door. I got up and opened it. Clyde came bursting onto my scene holding two cups of coffee in front of him and a brown sack between his teeth. He extended one of the coffees to me and said something.

"Clyde, I can't understand you. Didn't your mother teach you not to talk with your mouth full?"

He took the bag from his mouth. "Muffins," he said. "Where's Valerie?"

"She's out with some kind of flu."

"Yeah, I heard that's been going around."

"Sturgis should be here in a minute. Unfortunately," I said.

I was still pissed at him because of my house.

"Hey, you should be nicer to your CFO," Sturgis said as he came through the door. "Particularly if he's armed."

He turned to Clyde. "Hey, Clyde, good to see you." They bumped fists.

"Ah, muffins," he said looking at my desk. He took the one I wanted. "When's Jeffries supposed to be here?"

"He said 9:15 a.m. or so, depending on traffic," Clyde said. Jeffries was the designated driver that Parker & Simenon had appointed for our public offering. I suspected that this assignment did not bode well for his career.

At 9:45 a.m., we were still sitting there, looking at each other.

"There must have been an accident," Sturgis said, looking at his watch. "These guys are never late."

It was about lunchtime that we got the call from Jeffries' secretary. Where was he? Mr. Parker wanted to talk to him.

Sturgis started the calls. By two, we knew that Jeffries was going to be very late. Sturgis had been right. Jeffries had been delayed by an accident. His. Apparently, his car had suddenly veered off the road. It was totaled. So was Mr. Jeffries.

Clyde shook his head. "This is not good."

My threat level went from terrified to holy shit. If they were targeting the underwriters, what about Karen? I freaked out.

"You have to do something to protect my family." I was practically shouting.

"We don't even know it wasn't an accident, Harris."

"You don't believe that."

"Actually, no."

"How did these guys know who was handling the offering?"

"It was on the red herring," Sturgis said.

"No, it wasn't," Clyde said, a concerned note in his voice, "Only Parker & Simenon's name was on the red herring. Not Jeffries."

"And how did they know Jeffries was driving up here this morning?" I asked.

"I don't know." Sturgis said.

"What sources of information do they have? How sophisticated are they?"

Sturgis raised his voice. "I don't know, damn it?" He hit the desk hard.

I was starting to become unglued. I ran a hand through my hair.

"There's no way I'm going to let you put Karen at risk. I'll blow your damned operation before I let that happen." I was so agitated spittle was running down my chin. I wiped at it distractedly.

"Hey, you were the one who sent them away," Sturgis said anger suffusing his voice. "I told you we'd protect them."

"Where? In my former house?"

"Maybe it wouldn't have burned down."

"For God's sake, Sturgis, cut the crap. You need to send someone up there right now to be with them. These guys know how to get information and how to execute on it."

That was an unfortunate choice of words.

Chapter 44

"Hi, Jimmy. Mom and I are going stir crazy."

I'd finally reached Karen on my fourth call.

"We've done every spa treatment twice. And we're starting to get on each other's nerves. Even Bruno is surly.

"Karen, stop!"

"Jimmy, what is it?"

"Please just listen to me. I need for you and Mom to check out of your hotel right now."

"It's five o'clock in the afternoon. We'll check out first thing tomorrow morning?"

"Honey, you need to pack and leave right now." I was trying to avoid sounding hysterical. I may not have been wholly successful.

"My God, why?"

"Because Manny Comacho may know where you are."

"Jimmy, Manny Comacho is an idiot." Karen sounded adamant. "A violent idiot. But he's not going to find us in Mendocino."

"Please, Karen. Just do it for me." I was begging. "Comacho wouldn't be able to find you, but we're dealing with people who are much more dangerous. I'll explain everything later. But, right now, I need you to take care of yourself and Mom."

"Jimmy, you're beginning to scare me."

She had nothing on me. I was lapping that field.

"Good."

The line went silent.

"Do you have any cash left?" I asked.

"About $500."

"Great, find another hotel. Motel. Anywhere. At least five miles away. Don't use a credit card for anything from now on. Not food, not gas."

"But that will take all of our cash."

"Don't worry, I'll fix that. I have an FBI agent coming up to stay with you. He'll bring more cash."

"Where will you get the cash?"

"I have boxes of the stuff. Remember?"

"Okay. But, my God, Jimmy, do you think we need a body-guard?" She sounded stunned.

"Yes... I hope not. At least until we get a handle on what's going on."

"You're really scaring me now."

"I'm scared, too. When you've got a place, call me from a hard-line on 816-555-1623 and tell me where you are."

"Whose number is that?"

"It's an FBI cellphone. It's secure. I don't know if our cellphones are being bugged."

"What's going on?"

"Honey, not now. After we hang up, I want you and Mom to take the batteries out of your cellphones. You can't use them. Can you put Mom on for a second?"

"Hold on. She's out on the patio. 'Mom.'"

There was a second or two of silence.

"James."

"Hi, Mom. Are you having a good vacation?"

"Of course. I love Karen."

"How is Bruno doing?"

"Everyone needs a man around the house."

"Mom, you and Karen are going to move to a new hotel tonight."

"Absolutely not. I like this hotel. The avocado toast is divine."

"Mom, you have to do it. It's important. This is something

Karen needs to do. It's all going to sound strange, but just do what she says. Please."

"Oh, all right."

"Promise. Everything she says."

"James, I said I would. But I'm doing this for Karen."

"Great. Please put Karen back on."

"Jimmy, it may take a while to find a place. Mom needs special access and not many places will take Bruno. This crazy flu has shut down a lot of places around here."

I knew there was a flu epidemic. I just had other things on my mind. Samuel Johnson said the fear of being cut up into small pieces wonderfully focuses the mind.

"Jimmy, don't worry about us. We'll be okay. Just be careful."

"Honey, there are a dozen FBI agents around here, all protecting me."

Not one of whom would take a bullet, even in a Kevlar vest. Of course not. They had Plan B.

"I couldn't bear to see you hurt. Bruno needs a dad."

"Yeah, how is the little guy."

"He's doing fine. Do you want him to bark into the phone?" Thank goodness she hadn't lost her sense of humor. I had.

"And Jimmy." She paused. "I don't want to get married without you.

Aw.

Chapter 45

THE MOON SEEMED AS big as a house and looked like it was about to fall out of the sky. Kenneth Singer knew vaguely that it had to do with light refraction and atmospheric conditions, but it still amazed him. Well, there were some things they didn't teach you at Harvard. Probably at Yale. They probably had a whole course devoted to it.

It was cold. He had the windows rolled up and the front windshield defroster going. He was lulled by the sound. Chestnut Hill was beautiful in the early evening, with all the grand houses, but this wasn't a trip he was looking forward to. What a debacle the Wee Willy's investment had been.

Things had been going well, except for that. He had been sending the old ladies chocolate edibles every week. His mail reminded him of why Boston matrons didn't have orgies. Too many thank you notes.

Maybe they wanted to increase the amount he managed. Wee Willy's would come out okay when he could finally pursue the lawsuit. He would promise them that.

The car started to drift on the narrow road and the steering wheel bucked as a tire hit the rut at the side. His attention snapped back from his musing.

He hadn't been as forthcoming about Wee Willy's as he might have been. It was a little embarrassing and he had taken a risk. But it had been such a sweet deal. He had had to make a snap decision.

He had mentioned the problem in passing to Mrs. McKittrick. He had assured her that there would be no issue. She had asked about the delay and he had told her about the FBI. It wasn't his fault.

She hadn't said anything at the time, but now she wanted him at this meeting of the investment club. He guessed that was okay. But why did everyone have to meet at night?

He turned into the driveway of the big house. She was a sweet old lady. And their investment club had been sort of fun in its own way. They weren't sophisticated, but what could you expect.

He knocked on the heavy oak door. A gust of cold air made him pull his overcoat closer around him as the door opened.

"Mr. Singer. Mrs. McKittrick is expecting you," the maid said. She led him into the dining room. There was no one else there. He shed his topcoat and took his usual seat.

Maybe they had reset the time and he had overlooked the e-mail. There wasn't even a pot of tea. There was always tea.

"Mr. Singer." The voice startled him. Agnes McKittrick had slipped into the room. They had always gotten along great. He sometimes even kidded with the old girl. Now she seemed almost formal. He rose.

"Mrs. McKittrick." He walked over and pulled out the chair for her. She wasn't smiling. She sat and looked up at him.

"Mr. Singer, we are disappointed in you."

"I..."

"I am very angry. You've squandered $1,000,000 of our money. We want you to return it."

He collapsed into a chair. "I'm sorry. Can you say that again?"

"Don't make excuses, Mr. Singer. We want you to return the $1,000,000 you put into Wee Willy's. You didn't have the decency to tell us what was going on."

"I did tell you we had a problem and that I was in the process of resolving it."

"You mentioned it only vaguely."

"I didn't think it was that important."

"I've had my lawyer look into it. I've read a copy of the complaint you filed against them."

That was ugly. He had laid it on thick in that complaint.

"We'll get back the money back with interest, Mrs. McKittrick. I guarantee it."

"When?" Agnes McKittrick stared at him with hard eyes. There was something in them that made him uneasy.

Singer grimaced and made an open-handed gesture of uncertainty. "The FBI..."

"That, Mr. Singer is part of the problem. How could you get us involved in such a disreputable matter? I told you that we wanted privacy. Now you have the FBI involved in our affairs. That is most unacceptable."

"But you demanded we make the investment. You insisted."

"I remember no such thing. We are just widows. You told us it was a utensils company."

"Mrs. McKittrick, this is a terrible misunderstanding."

"We want all of our money back, Mr. Singer." She spoke quietly but with emphasis.

This was not a sweet old lady. There was something distinctly menacing in her quiet words.

"I can cash out your other investments, but getting back the $1,000,000 will take some time."

"I see, Mr. Singer. And during all of that time the FBI will be looking into this investment you've made for us. And perhaps into our private affairs. No. We want you to give us our money and erase our involvement. Our name will be in no way associated with this company."

"Mrs. McKittrick, I don't have $1,000,000."

"I don't believe you fully understand, Mr. Singer."

Her voice was soft but the words sounded like stones being dropped on the floor.

"We want our money back within two weeks. And we want you to disappear from our lives. You have caused us difficulty. Our name will not be associated in any way with anything you have done. Please see to it."

"That's impossible. I can't get $1,000,000 in two weeks."

"I would hope you can, Mr. Singer. We may seem to you like harmless old ladies, but we do have relationships that could make it difficult for you. Make problems I do not believe you want to confront. Now, please go."

The drive back was even more unpleasant. He didn't like this. He remembered her late husband and his alleged associates. Surely, she wasn't threatening him with physical harm. No, of course not. But the image wouldn't go away. He was so upset he didn't even consider the management fees he'd lost. He spent a disturbed night from which he woke up exhausted.

It wasn't until late the next afternoon that the thought struck him. What a great idea. He could sell the Wee Willy's deal to one of his investment banking buddies in New York. He could pitch it as high risk, high reward.

Yeah, what fun it would be to own your own pot company. Kind of like owning a winery, but cooler. A few million dollars to those guys was tip money. Maybe he could even keep some for himself. He rubbed his hands together.

Singer picked up the phone and started calling. He reminded himself that he needed to find out what was going on at Wee Willy's.

Chapter 46

"THAT'S ACTUALLY A BRIGHT idea," Sturgis said. I was pleased he finally appreciated my insights. Unfortunately, I had no idea what he meant. I hoped Clyde did.

"The muscle, represented by Mr. Comacho, is getting a lot of information from somewhere. Sophisticated information on a real-time basis. If we can get ahead of Comacho, he may lead us to where we want to go. And if we take him out, it may make the cartel change direction and provide some opportunity."

"That sounds right," Clyde said.

"If they think they got Jimmy and the investment banker, then there are only three obvious targets left." Sturgis was really into this. "Those are Karen, Clyde and me."

"Why would they want to take you out?"

"First, it's who they are. And, they need to close this down. They can't be sure who might push the public offering."

That made sense in a perverse kind of way.

"I'm a hard target. We'll make sure Clyde is a hard target. You, Jimmy, are dead and will disappear."

I was counting on my fingers. I didn't like his arithmetic.

"You can't use Karen, damn it. I told you that." I may have spoken loudly and in a high voice. Several glasses in the room shattered.

Sturgis held his hands up in surrender. "I'm not going to use Karen. I'm going to use her identity and her credit cards."

"Explain."

"You were right. They may be able to track credit cards. Karen and your Mom will drop off the grid with the guy I've sent up to stay with them. She'll give us her cellphone and her credit cards."

I made a mental note to speak to Sturgis about any charges on the cards. You can't trust the FBI.

"I'll get a female agent and a protection unit to take the phone and cards and use them somewhere else. Somewhere we can set up a contained perimeter. The female agent will look something like Karen, at least from a distance."

"You've never met Karen."

"No. Do you have a picture? Or better yet, a video?"

"I'll get you one."

"When Comacho tries to hit our agent, we'll take him down."

"Boy, there are a lot of maybes," Clyde said.

"I know. And we can't be sure of the timing. But these guys have to move fast. I'm betting they will try the easy target first and do it quickly."

"If you take down Comacho, you don't think he'll talk to you, do you?" I said.

"Of course not. He's an idiot, but he's not insane. Maybe he'll have a burner phone. Even a computer."

"How far will that get you?"

"A lot farther than where we are now."

"It's your show," I said finally, "but you've got to get Karen and my mom safe."

"My guy's on the way. He'll be there today. We'll move them again tonight. By the way, what was in the package you asked him to take?"

"Just some personal stuff Karen will need." Like money.

"Don't do it again. We're not your errand boys."

"I won't." I hoped I would never have to. "Um, Special Agent Sturgis," I said in a hesitant voice.

"What?"

"Do you think maybe you could get someone who looks like me too?"

"Absolutely not. No FBI agent would dare look like you. Besides, you're dead. Stay that way."

Chapter 47

THIS IS HARD TO believe. We finally got lucky.

The cockamamie plan actually worked, although it took four days of sitting on pins and needles. Even the FBI didn't screw it up.

Sturgis spent half an hour talking to one of his agents on the phone. He was so chuffed he told me all about it. He was really happy. I think he smiled.

As Sturgis recounted the conversation, my mind created the tale. He's a lousy story teller. The man was a dot short of an exclamation point.

Comacho made the attempt in Lake Tahoe. He wore all black down to his sneakers and had smeared dark lines down his face. The invisible man at night. He was proud he had been given such an important task by Senor Hernandez. Senor Hernandez was a big man.

The woman had not been hard to find. He was given her exact location in a text on his cellphone. It was a six-hour drive.

Comacho had spent the last night and day looking over the area. It was smart to be prepared. There was a dirt path through a deeply wooded area from the road to the place where he could shoot the woman. It would not be hard with the 50 mm hunting scope mounted on the .30-06 caliber Springfield bolt-action rifle Senor Hernandez had given him. He liked this gun. It felt good in his hands.

It was more difficult in the dark, but he found the place to pull the car off the road where no one would see it. It was about two hundred yards to the opening in the woods where the path began.

The night was cloudy and a light rain was falling. He was cold. His thin nylon jacket was uninsulated. The woods were very dark, filled with the noisy silence of nature.

The only unnatural sound was Manny Comacho. Comacho was thick, with large hands and feet. He had never been in the woods at night. He wondered if there were snakes. He was afraid of snakes.

He carried a flashlight. That was a mistake. The light destroyed his night vision and announced his presence. He kind of knew that, but he didn't care. He didn't like snakes and no one else was around.

The path was rocky and uneven. The rain made it slippery and it was hard to make good time. Sometimes the trees grew across the path and cast odd shadows. Comacho was jumpy. He didn't like being in the woods at night.

He slipped and went down hard on his elbow. He cursed under his breath as he struggled up. Mud caked his pretty new shoes and his feet were wet. Camacho angrily pulled the rifle to his chest and carefully examined it with the flashlight. No mud had fouled it.

Every time the bushes rustled, he paused in mid stride and moved the flashlight nervously to the sound. After a minute or two, he continued down the path.

He was not a quiet man. He never needed to be quiet. The noise he made obstructed most of the sounds.

The sudden cracking of a branch made him turn and bring the rifle around from his back. He crouched and stared into the darkness, the rifle gripped across his chest with his finger on the trigger.

He slowly brought the rifle to his shoulder and pointed it at the place where the noise had come from. He held the flashlight against the side of the stock and moved the rifle slowly back and forth across the trees. Sweat trickled down his back. He shivered involuntarily.

It was silent. But he felt like there were eyes staring at him from the woods. He stayed there for several minutes until the burning in his calves made him stand.

He shook out his muscles, took a final nervous look around and started on.

Chapter 48

IT TOOK HIM THREE quarters of an hour to reach the little hill he had selected. His breath was ragged. It had seemed closer in the daytime.

He slid off his backpack and bent over with his hands on his knees. He put his head down and tried to calm himself. He would have to be steady to shoot the woman from here.

Nothing was in sight from the hill but a small group of cabins in a clearing in the woods about two hundred yards away. There were lights on in three of them. People crossed back and forth in front of the large windows. Behind one, a young woman sat alone at a table, playing solitaire.

He slipped on his backpack and started up a pine tree with the rifle hanging over his shoulder. He didn't want to come any closer to the cabin and he needed more height. A city boy, dressed in black, shinnying up a tree in the forest at night.

Comacho's breath was labored with the effort. The sweat glistened on his forehead in the moonlight. Apparently, tree climbing was not a big sport in the barrio.

"Can you believe it? They caught him climbing a fucking tree," Sturgis laughed.

He had almost made it to the first limb when six FBI agents braced him, rifles leveled. They must have looked like the army, in Kevlar vests and full combat gear, armed to the teeth.

"FBI. Do not move. Manny Comacho. You are under arrest."

It was a pretty easy takedown, except for the small incident. Comacho had both arms around the tree and his knees and cheek were pressed into it.

The FBI left him clinging to the tree until he got tired and dropped off. One of the agents tripped on a tree root backing away from the spot where Comacho fell. Fortunately, no one was injured in the accidental discharge, although there were a couple of really pissed horned owls. The shot brought three FBI agents surging from the cabins, guns drawn.

Comacho sprained his ankle and broke two fingers. There were streaks of blood on his face where the bark had scraped his cheek.

It was only an eight-foot drop and the ground was soft. But it's awkward when you have a rifle between your legs. There may also have been damage to other vulnerable parts. They rolled him over on his stomach and handcuffed him as he screamed for a doctor.

The whole thing was enough to give you faith. Maybe not in the government. But in a just God. Although I have to say, he took his time.

They got Comacho's burner phone from his pocket. He had fallen on it but it did more harm to him than to the phone. Solid Chinese manufacturing.

His car was located the next morning parked off a dirt road about half a mile from the tree. There was a personal computer in it. They towed it in and took the car to pieces.

The blood had crusted on Comacho's face by the time of the interview. He was yelling about police brutality when he could catch his breath from calling for his lawyer. It looked like Mr. Comacho was going to be out of my hair for a long time. Attempted murder of a Federal police officer is frowned upon in some circles.

And maybe the good guys would get lucky and tie the ballistics from Comacho's rifle into the investment banker's murder. The police had concluded that a tire had been shot out, although no bullet or cartridge case yet had been recovered.

Then there was something else.

"They found a kilo of cocaine in a hidden compartment in the wheel well of Comacho's car," Sturgis said with real glee in his voice. "Of course, he had never seen it before. Someone must have left it there during the night to frame him."

It seems the boy was multitasking. His mother would have been proud.

Chapter 49

"WELL, I'LL BE DAMNED," Sturgis said putting down the phone and turning to Clyde. "It must be Christmas."

Now I knew it wasn't Christmas and so did Clyde. More like Thanksgiving. But you don't look askance at an FBI agent bearing gifts. You look at him quizzically.

"That was no one other than John Campion. He wants to come up tomorrow and talk about the sale. I do believe we're about to have some fun."

Actually, the fun I had been planning all night was Karen's homecoming. I missed her. And I was really horny. Sturgis had agreed that Karen should come home after Thanksgiving if she was willing to let the FBI protect her. I intended to protect her myself. Perhaps by throwing myself on top of her.

All I had to do was to figure out where we were going to do that. Which might lead unavoidably to our having a discussion about our ex-house. Which in turn might lead to an impediment to our homecoming celebration. Oh well, guess I could pet Bruno if he remembered me.

Sturgis wouldn't let me come to the meeting with John Campion, me being dead. But he did let me listen over the intercom.

I knew John Campion from my former life. He had represented Guy Mason last year in his divorce from the late Janet. He didn't like me.

Mr. Campion is six feet, two inches. He was well turned out in his tailor-made, pin-striped suits. I'll bet he has his own fabric pattern. His gray hair was beautifully cut. I know, I peeked when he came in.

"Mr. Campion," Sturgis said heartily. "It's an honor. I know of your firm and your reputation." Sturgis was laying the sugar on with a trowel. I hoped Campion wouldn't lapse into a diabetic coma.

"It's nice to meet you, Mr. Sturgis." Campion turned in a rather shortened gesture. "This is William Blough, one of our associates." The young man had floated in, pulled by Campion's wake.

"I appreciate your coming all the way up here. May I get you coffee or tea? I also brought in some Danish from our local bakery. They're quite good."

"Just coffee, thanks."

"Cream? Sugar?"

"Black."

"Mr...?"

"Blough."

"Yes, sorry. Mr. Blough?"

"Nothing, thanks."

"Excuse me for a moment. My secretary is still out with the flu."

"Sure, we're having the same problem. Very disruptive."

"I'll be right back."

"Make sure you take good notes," Campion said, turning on the young associate when Sturgis had left the room. "This is important. I don't want you to disappoint me again."

"But you..."

"I don't want to hear excuses," Campion snarled.

Sturgis pushed the coffee room door open with his foot, two cups of coffee in his hands. He winked at me going down the hall on his way past.

———————

"Now, Mr. Campion, how can I help you?"

"First, let me say, we were sorry to hear about Mr. Harris. A fine lawyer. We worked together. I liked him."

Aw shucks.

"A tragedy," Sturgis said.

"Indeed."

That was short lived.

"You know, of course, Mr. Sturgis, my clients have made an offer for your company. We were disappointed your board wasn't more responsive. It was a very fair offer. I came up here myself to stress my client's interest in acquiring Wee Willy's."

"I'm only the CFO. This is hardly my company. But I'm happy to discuss the situation with you."

"I assume you are in charge."

"Yes, I suppose so. For the time being, at least."

"Then that's fine. Please."

"This may be an opportune time for your client," Sturgis said. "You know our primary concern was the financial viability of your offer."

"Yes. And I'm here to assure you of that. This is one of our most important clients. We are outside general counsel for all their U.S. business. We have represented them for many years."

That was interesting.

"I can assure you they will have no problem financing this acquisition." Ball in our court.

"I'm certain you are correct, Mr. Campion. And, coming from you, I would require nothing else. But you do understand I need to have actual financial information to present to our board." Volley back across the net.

"Yes. And my clients have authorized me to provide it if we can come to satisfactory terms. But time is of the essence for my clients." Set and match.

"Mr. Campion, I'm curious. Can you tell me how Wee Willy's came to your client's attention? We're just a small business. In this little town."

"My clients have been involved in the marijuana industry from the time it became legal. They have several companies and they are one of the major domestic hemp farmers. Campboll Water has a large farming operation in the Central Valley."

I could picture Sturgis writing all this down. I just hope he wasn't drooling on his notes.

"Obviously, my clients pay a lot of attention to what is happening in the business. And they were impressed with what they heard about Wee Willy's. You are doing some innovative marketing."

"It's nice of you to say so. May I take you on a tour?"

"Not right now. Perhaps later."

"Then, let me review our financial position and marketing plans."

"We've read the prospectus for your public offering. Is there anything you need to add?"

"No. It's all there. Then perhaps we can talk about the possibility of a deal over lunch. I've ordered in sandwiches. We set up everything in our conference room. At some point, I'd would like to know how you intend for us to fit into your existing operations."

"Yes. And you can take us on that tour you promised."

It went quiet. Sturgis hadn't bothered to connect me with the conference room. Nor had he sent a sandwich my way. But I did see them go out towards the greenhouse after an hour. They appeared to be in high spirits.

I was hungry.

Chapter 50

"WELL, THAT'S ABOUT IT," Sturgis said, as the door creaked. I could just make out his voice. He and Campion were still a long way from the intercom. But we were back on the air.

"Your facilities are impressive, but I'm surprised you don't have more people," Campion said, the voices becoming stronger. I could hear chairs scrapping.

"We're trying to hold our expenses down during this start-up period to invest in the business. I've been with the company a short time myself, but I realized they weren't managing their cash flow very well."

"That does bring up an issue I wanted to discuss. You asked how Wee Willy's would be integrated with our other businesses."

"I appreciate your coming back to that. I was hoping I might be able to stay on."

"Normally, Mr. Sturgis, we would be anxious to have you. But my clients want to centralize their financial operations. I hope you understand."

This was where Sturgis gave his Academy Award performance. "Sure."

In that one word he infused professionalism, disappointment and acceptance.

"Let me assure you however, you will be well taken care of." Campion hurried on. "My clients have authorized me to negotiate a generous closing bonus and an exceptional severance package. I am sure you will be pleased."

It was the time-honored corporate strategy. Bribe the help.

"No problem." Sturgis's voice was noticeably brighter. "But the board will be concerned about the other people. After all, they live here. And will this be good for the town?"

I was proud of John Campion. He sold his deal like a horse trader extolling the virtues of a horse he just rescued from the slaughter house. He was fluent and convincing. He painted a picture of his client's operations and the opportunities they presented. It was fulfilling. It was particularly fulfilling to the FBI.

Finally, Mr. Campion wound down.

"That really is impressive. May I speak openly to you about your offer, Mr. Campion?" Sturgis said it suggestively.

"Certainly. I believe we have that kind of relationship," said the Big Bad Wolf to Red Riding Hood, licking his chops. He didn't know Red Riding Hood had a gun.

"I don't think you need to increase your price. But if you could provide me with some bank references, I think I can sell your offer. In fact, I'm sure I can."

"That is good news, Mr. Sturgis. I have been authorized to give you the copy of a Letter of Credit for the full purchase price of the acquisition, upon the signing of the Letter of Intent."

"The board will also want to close promptly. Forty-five days?"

"No problem."

"We're talking all cash?"

"Yes."

"Then, when can we get a revised Letter of Intent?"

"You'll have it to you before the end of the day."

"And the Letter of Credit?"

"When I get back a signed copy."

"And may I have a separate e-mail on the details of my bonus and severance package. After I look them over, perhaps we can talk further." The little devil.

Sturgis waved at Campion as he drove away, then turned towards the office with a smile so broad I was afraid his ears would fall off. I met him at the door. We bumped fists. "You were fantastic," I said.

"I thought I was pretty good."

"With all that information, you'll be able to really get into the cartel's operations and banking."

"Yep."

"Won't there be a problem with closing. What's going to happen when Campion starts digging into Wee Willy's financial records? We made up all that stuff for the red herring?"

"Not to worry. We have people who will create anything we need. Mr. Campion will be pleased with Wee Willy's. I can assure you of that. And now that we know that Campion & Gilbert are involved so deeply, after we close, we're going to subpoena every record they have."

"What about attorney-client privilege?"

"They're assisting in an ongoing criminal activity. It doesn't apply. I think Mr. Campion is going to have a lot of non-billable time soon. Maybe we can make that permanent. I really don't like lawyers."

He looked me directly in the eyes. "Except Clyde."

I chose to ignore that.

"You'll probably get a medal."

"The FBI doesn't give medals."

"Come on, you know what I mean."

"Maybe they'll make me Supervising Special Agent of the Honolulu office."

I sensed that the choo choo to take the FBI out of my life was emerging from the tunnel.

"So, can I leave?"

"Oh, you can't leave. We really do have to close the deal."

"Why?"

"Two reasons," Sturgis said. "We need the forty-five days to investigate all these business and banking leads and see what's up. It will also give us time to line up our subpoenas and search warrants."

"That makes sense. Reason two?"

"We need to get our money back. And, of course, my bonus."

"You're not actually going to give them Wee Willy's, are you?"

"How can we do that? We don't own it." As if that made a difference to the FBI. "We'll just take their money. But look on the bright side of it. We'll have forty-five more days together. You're dead. You've got to stay that way." Sturgis sounded almost chipper.

"Can Karen and I go someplace else?" The thought of having to spend forty-five more days with Special Agent Sturgis was a punishment no civilized man should endure. Nor should I.

"We'll have to vet any place you choose. It needs to be far away. But sure, why not."

"What happens after forty-five days?"

"We're through. We're gone."

"What about me?"

"What about you, Mr. Harris?"

"You know, the Singer lawsuit. The murder investigation."

"Those aren't important."

"Yes, they are."

"I meant to us."

"But you're going to tell the police about the cartel? I mean, they still think I murdered Willy." I was getting a little excited.

"You wouldn't expect us to compromise a major ongoing investigation. Please, Mr. Harris."

He patted me on the shoulder.

"I'm sure you'll figure something out. And of course, you'll still have Wee Willy's."

He laughed. It wasn't an entirely pleasant sound.

Chapter 51

I'VE ALWAYS LOVED THE holidays. The months from October the last through January the first are my favorite time of the whole year. Then, even in California there are a few days of moody weather. I like moody weather. It's a nice change from the summer reruns. I think they record one weather forecast on the first day of summer, then rerun it for three months.

Like the weather, our days at the ranch were an endless repetition of Groundhog Day. With rare moments of terrifying excitement. But it was the endless repetition that could drive a sane man crazy. So I was crazy. I mean I was sane.

Finally, it was Thanksgiving. Of all the holidays, I love Thanksgiving the most. Maybe it's because I've known so many turkeys.

Or because the stores are not yet trying to sell me everything in the known universe. Sure, Christmas is great. I believe in Santa, but how many Santas can be around before they start to stretch their credibility. And "Jingle Bells" gets boring after the first dozen times you hear it. By the way, did you know "Jingle Bells" was written by J.P. Morgan's uncle?

My mother took us to Christmas Eve services when we were little. I would have liked it more if there was snow. I mean I enjoyed "White Christmas," although I never figured out what Bing Crosby saw in Rosemary Clooney.

So, Thanksgiving is the best. Mom did Thanksgiving well. How she had the time to roast the turkey and bake pecan pies I can't imagine. I also never thought about it. We were all always sprawled on the living room floor watching the Macy's parade until we had to set the table.

It's funny what we remember. The smells. How can you remember smells?

Mom put on the show, but Dad oversaw the turkey. He taught me how to carve. First, he would sharpen his knife, then start with the drumsticks. He always saved me a wing.

My aunt and uncle would arrive with platters of food. They also brought their two kids. My cousins were nerds. All they were interested in was computers. I never understood a thing they said.

I mean, computers are okay but girls have more moving parts. That's probably why they are multi-millionaires and I'm having Thanksgiving with people who have guns.

Thanksgiving at the ranch left me decidedly short of joy. If there hadn't been turkey, at least I think it was turkey, I would have missed it entirely.

Then again, it was better than Halloween. Have you ever been to an FBI Halloween party? For your peace of mind, avoid it.

Gloria Ramirez came as Bonnie Parker. My roommate, Watkins, came as Clyde Barrow. Everyone had a favorite criminal. The Dapper Don was there, as was Willy Sutton.

One agent even came as Al Pacino playing Scarface. I thought that showed imagination. This guy wasn't going to get much exercise on his career path if he kept showing imagination.

Sturgis came as J. Edgar Hoover. I came as myself. I thought that was criminal enough.

It was really great fun if you forgot the weapons were real. No one was killed, although there was a tense moment when J. Edgar arrested Scarface. To Sturgis's credit, J. Edgar hardly tiptoed at all.

We gathered for the Thanksgiving festivities in the main house at our usual hour, dressed to the nines. Unfortunately, that was on a scale of twelve.

Before we dug in, Sturgis gave us a pep talk. Thank God everyone had checked their guns at the door. I wasn't sure whether I would have committed murder or suicide. But then again, I was already dead, the fact of which Sturgis often reminded me. From my standpoint, I was giving my all, but not my thanks.

There was a rapt discussion over dinner of the stopping power of the .357 handgun. I think several of my fellows made a note to add one to their Christmas list.

This led naturally into a spirited dispute about the authenticity of the FBI. Myself, I'm a fan of *NYPD Blue*.

Ours wasn't exactly a family gathering. I missed Karen and Bruno a lot. I hoped they were having more fun with their FBI bodyguard. If absence makes the heart grow fonder, this togetherness was driving me nuts.

Chapter 52

I WAS LYING THERE, looking at Karen's face in the morning sunlight that pushed in through the curtains. I never tire of looking at the line of her chin or her freckled nose.

Her eyes were closed and the sheet rose and fell with her breathing. She made little sounds. Then Bruno started barking and scratching at the door.

Things were back, not to normal, but something like it. As normal as it gets for a guy who's dead and who's home and office have burned to the ground. And who is hiding out in a rented house.

Karen stirred and opened her eyes. Then she rolled over towards me and brushed my cheek with her hand. "Good morning, lover," she said with a great smile. I don't think anyone has ever said anything nicer to me. I know I'm a cornball romantic, but there it is.

Karen had come back to San Buenasara the day after Thanksgiving. It had taken a few days to find a place.

I found a small house near Santa Margurita on Craig's List. Santa Margurita is a little town off the highway between San Luis Obispo and Atascadero. It makes San Buenasara look cosmopolitan.

I chose it because I had never heard of it. I assumed that no one else had heard of it either. It was a good place to hide out while the FBI did its thing.

It's actually a nice little town if you put the emphasis on little. Even Sturgis approved. Since I still had my snout firmly in the

FBI's trough, money wasn't a problem. Which was good, because I had no intention of touching any more of the money that I had in the boxes until we knew a lot more about what was going on. Sturgis was providing us cash for expenses.

It was a cute little place. Some people in Arizona owned it. Probably Mom and Dad's old place that couldn't be sold because of the recession. It even had indoor plumbing.

You had to overlook some rust stains in the bathtub, but water actually came out of the taps. We were on a rural back road. It was at least 200 yards to the nearest neighbor.

It could use a paint job and some remodeling, but it would do, given the alternatives. I rented the house for a month in one of Sturgis's agent's names, cash in advance.

Karen kicked off the covers. She was naked. It gave me an instant hard-on. Karen noticed and giggled. "Down boy," she said as she kissed the end of my protuberance. I would have been more upset if we hadn't made love twice last night.

The air was heavy and sweet with the smell of new mown grass. And there were birds singing. I felt a sense of joy. It surprised me. I had missed that feeling for a long time.

Bruno bounded into the room as Karen opened the door to get to the bathroom. "Here boy," I said patting the bed beside me. Bruno and I are close. He allows me to pet him when Karen isn't around. Or Clyde. Or the mailman.

After Bruno made three futile tries at leaping onto the mattress, I leaned down and scooped him up. He licked my hands. Absence makes the heart grow fonder. I gave him a big kiss on the forehead, and started scratching him behind the ears.

"Miss me, big guy?" Bruno didn't respond.

"Hey, I'm jealous," Karen said coming through the doorway. She slipped into a yellow robe.

"Come over here and I'll scratch you behind the ears too."

Karen walked over and sat on the edge of the bed. She started petting Bruno as I scratched him. I now know the face of contentment.

"We really have to talk about what's going on," I said over Bruno's back. "Once Sturgis closes his deal, we'll be twisting in the wind. I don't trust him."

"We do have to talk, honey, but not now. Let's just be quiet. Bruno needs our attention." I leaned across Bruno and kissed her. I can multitask with the best of them.

Chapter 53

WE WERE SITTING IN the Old Mill on Main Street. We had been in the house for three boring days. It was the first time we had ventured out. Karen didn't like the idea, but I insisted. I felt like we had to go out sometimes. We would make it late in the morning. After breakfast, but before lunch.

I kept low in the car while Karen drove. I was on edge. I'm a friendly guy. I love seeing my friends. We knew no one. Now I dreaded seeing a familiar face. I hadn't realized how jumpy it would make me.

And when there are only 2,000 people in town, it kind of limits the choice of restaurants. But the Old Mill was pretty good. I mean, it wasn't The Lilly Pad. But then nothing is The Lilly Pad.

The town was quiet in the winter sun. Winter kept the farmers in. There was no extra money.

We got lucky. No one else was in the restaurant. We relaxed a bit.

Karen's French toast wasn't artful, but it was substantial. I'll never understand how the girl remains so sleek. My poached eggs and dry toast tasted like cardboard. There were some downsides in having Karen back.

Karen had not approved of my diet in her absence. Pizza and soda contain all the essential vitamins and minerals, if, now and then, you have a cheeseburger. And a little extra weight looks good on a guy, even if Karen had taken to pinching the delicate folds of my stomach.

Karen raised her fork. She pointed it at me as she spoke.

"There's no reason we still can't sell Wee Willy's to Mr. Singer," she said. She looked down again and cut a small bite. She lifted it delicately to her mouth and chewed.

"The FBI has been running the business to keep up the façade," she said. "If anything, the brand and trademarks are more valuable than before."

"I think you're right. We need to wait on the Feds. It won't be too long. Sturgis set the closing for forty-five days. I'll call Singer and get the ball rolling as soon as I can."

"Jimmy, what about Willy?"

I spread my hands on the table, face up. "I just don't know. The sheriff did interview me again a couple of months ago. But apparently things have really slowed down. After the FBI shooed them off, I haven't heard hide nor hair from them."

"I guess that's good."

"But my friend Sid the cop keeps following me around, so I know they haven't forgotten me."

I stopped abruptly.

"Darn it!"

"Jimmy, what's wrong?'

"I promised Sid I would call him when I went someplace. I forgot. I better call him right now. I don't want the police to think I made a run for it."

"You can't tell him where we are."

"No, but I can tell him why we are and promise I'll come back. At least the police won't issue an All-Points Bulletin."

"What did the sheriff want when she interviewed you?"

"Just routine. Where when and who. You would have been proud of me. I was charming and sincere. But I wish the FBI would give them the information on the drug cartel."

"Why won't they?"

"Ongoing investigation. Sturgis is being an ass."

"But you can tell them."

"Yeah, I will. I just don't know how to prove it unless the FBI tells her it's true. I don't think 'no comment' will cut it. But what about the house?" I said changing the subject.

"What about the house?" she repeated.

"We've got to have a place to live. Do you want to rebuild?"

"Yes," she said without pausing.

"Well, then, I do too. Let's find a house to rent and call Nate." Nate Rocco was our friend and an architect. "It will be nice to have something to look forward to. I guess I'll have to hustle up some clients."

Karen went back to her French toast.

"Oh, I forgot to tell you," I said. "The FBI hired us to do the legal work for Wee Willy's. Did I mention the public offering?"

"You're joking."

"No, really. I'll explain later. But Sturgis likes Clyde so much he asked him to handle the sale of the company."

"But there is no sale."

"Well, there won't be a transfer, but they have to do all the legal work so it doesn't look suspicious. I figure the FBI will owe us $30,000 or $40,000."

"Will they pay?"

"Unless they find out about the money."

"Of course they'll find out about the money. You'll have to bill them for the work."

"Not that money."

"What money?"

"The $1,000,000 in small bills we buried in the backyard."

"Ah."

Chapter 54

"MR. STURGIS?" THE MAN said. He was in jeans and a clean flannel shirt. He was of average height and slight of build. One of the temples of his glasses had been mended with scotch tape.

The only thing that distinguished him was the laminated card on a lanyard around his neck. The card said Warren Heath. Inspector. Occupational Safety and Health Administration with an official seal on it.

Valerie had announced that a man from OSHA was in the lobby requesting to meet with him.

"Yes."

"Are you in charge of this company?"

"Yes, I am."

"No doubt, you are aware of the rules and regulations adopted by OSHA governing the operation of agricultural enterprises such as this one."

"With some of them. I'm sure there are many I don't know about."

"My name is Warren Heath. We are doing an unannounced inspection of your facility today."

"Why?"

"Mr. Sturgis, we need to be sure you are adequately protecting your employees. I know you understand the importance of that."

"Of course I do. But could we make this inspection at another time? We have a lot going on at the moment."

"The entire purpose of the inspection is to do so unannounced. We need to be certain the company is complying. I'm afraid it can't be arranged at your convenience."

"Mr. eh..."

"Heath."

"You don't understand."

"No, frankly, I don't."

"You can't do this now."

"I most certainly can." His voice rose. "I am an official of the United States government and I am specifically empowered to do exactly this."

"Look, you're interfering with a major operation here. There are things I can't tell you. But you are in danger of doing something that could damage us, and severely harm your career."

"Are you threatening me?"

"No. No. I just can't explain. It is highly restricted information."

"Mr. Sturgis. I walked through your facility on a casual basis on my way in to see you. I can tell you, you have serious OSHA issues. So serious, it could cause me to shut down your operation."

"You can't do that."

"I saw evidence of the exposure of your workers to unacceptable levels of chemicals. People working without appropriate protective coverings. Examples of inappropriate disposal of waste materials. In fact, Mr. Sturgis, this is one of the most egregious violations of the law that I have ever witnessed."

"You don't understand."

"You've said that before. I wanted to make a more thorough inspection to assure myself of the validity of my observations, but your uncooperative attitude causes me even deeper concerns."

"This operation is unorthodox. It has been approved by the government."

"The responsibility for workers safety is part of the Department of Labor. I have never seen or heard of a business that is allowed to jeopardize worker's safety. Ever."

"But this isn't a business."

"Please, Mr. Sturgis, that is the most outlandish comment I have ever heard. You have been in business for over a year. You have people producing products. Mind you, products that I personally think are harmful and should have never been approved by any right-thinking government. I have seen your advertising. What you are doing is not legal under the Federal law. But that does not excuse you from complying with the rules and regulations Federal law imposes on you."

"Is there anything I can do to make this go away?" Sturgis envisioned his entire operation being compromised. He was growing desperate.

"If that is an allusion to a bribe, Mr. Sturgis, I will have you arrested."

"Good lord, Heath, that's not what I meant. Who can I talk to?"

"Me."

"I mean your supervisor."

"Certainly. I will give you a referral. But I will have to close your plant pending the resolution of that discussion."

———

It took two days of frantic conversations that reached high into the Federal government to mediate the issues. And it brought a great deal of attention to Wee Willy's which Sturgis did not appreciate. The Assistant Director was starting to nibble around the budget for the operation. That wasn't good.

"Fucking government."

———

And that was before the call from the mayor.

"Tony, we haven't met, but I was a great supporter of Willy Witkowski and his business."

"Thank you, Mr. Mayor." To his credit, Special Agent Anthony Sturgis was suspicious. "What can I do for you?"

"Oh, no. I want to be of service to you. In this time of recession, Wee Willy's is an important element of our economy. Although, I hear you have downsized your workforce."

"Sadly, that is true. We are still in a start-up phase and our re-sources and capital just did not keep up with our expenses."

"That is unfortunate. One reason I'm calling, Tony, is that we have had a lot of complaints about the impact of your business on other businesses in your area. And I have to say, there have been complaints on the odors originating from your greenhouse."

Was OSHA back?

"Mr. Mayor, we have always enjoyed your support. There are other interests that have been abusing the environment by over-spraying. These avocado interests. And yes, it has impacted us. We cannot afford the air scrubbers we want to install. But it also impacts everyone in our community."

"It has also been a concern."

"Smell is a problem. But we are an agricultural community here. If we had a pig farm and someone built next door, smell would be a problem. We need agriculture."

"Yes, I am certainly aligned with the farmers."

"As you say, we are new." The mayor didn't say that, but hell. "I believe if we can simply have time and your support, we will be a major contributor to employment and revenue for the city."

"I also believe that, Tony."

"Mr. Mayor, how can we contribute to insuring your continued support?"

"Well..."

What had he come to?

Chapter 55

THE GENERAL STORE ON Main Street was once the center of Santa Margurita. Those days were long past. That was assured when the new Ralph's opened ten miles away in the mega mall off the 101.

The paint was peeling and the steps creaked. We thought it wouldn't last the thirty days we had rented it for. You could buy nails and ax handles and a few basic supplies. It was our shop of choice because it was no one else's.

The pinto beans filled a big barrel by the front counter that had been worn by 100 years of use. An old, balding man with dentures, in a collarless button-up shirt and round, rimless glasses, stood behind it. His apron reached down to the floor. The cash register would have brought top dollar in an antique sale.

I stayed home most of the time, being dead, and Karen did the shopping. I couldn't figure out how the general store stayed in business. I hoped it wasn't drug money. That would be a problem. So, I checked.

As it turned out, a young techie couple had bought it. They were making a fortune on the internet in the back-to-basics movement. The store was their logo and centerpiece. Life was weird, even in little Santa Margurita.

We didn't go out a lot after that first foray to the Old Mill. I was pretty confident the cartel wasn't looking for us. Karen didn't think I had a lot of basis for that conclusion so she wasn't about to take any unnecessary risks, like shopping at the big market.

It was our third week and we were both going a little stir crazy. The only happy one was Bruno. He liked having us around all the time. It's good to have the help available.

Karen was out shopping for beans and pasta. Pasta, in the case of our general store, meant packaged spaghetti. The store didn't feature an extensive choice of brands. The spaghetti was in the one row of foodstuffs by the tomato sauce.

The good news was, you didn't spend a lot of time mulling your choices. Karen's shopping trips took about half an hour, including a ten-minute drive both ways.

When she walked back into the house, she looked flustered. She put the paper bag down on the counter and turned to me with her mouth drawn into a tight line.

"What's wrong?"

"I don't know. When I left the store there weren't a lot of people around. Just a couple of cars parked along the street. But this truck drove by me very slowly. I think the driver looked at me closely."

"It was just a farmer. You're a hot babe. I would have looked at you too."

"It wasn't a farmer, Jimmy. The truck was new and shiny. The man might have been Mexican. He was certainly Latino. I didn't get a good look at him because I ducked down behind the car."

"What do you think we should do?"

"I'm not sure. I do know that I'm scared."

"I guess we better stay low. Do we need anything?"

"More toilet paper. We're almost out. And more food."

"Maybe you should go to another market. Drive up to Atascadero or somewhere. Buy enough for the rest of the month. I'll go with you."

"You shouldn't be out."

"I'll wear my fake mustache. Or at least a baseball cap. I'll stay in the car."

It was some mark of how scared Karen was that she didn't argue. We chose the following Thursday. We drove to Templeton, which is above Atascadero and off the main road. I figured we were safe. We found a small market and we bought everything we needed for the remaining eight days. And more. Sometimes I think my mother was Jewish.

We got back on the 101. We were past Atascadero and almost to our turn off when Karen went rigid.

"It's him."

I turned in my seat. Three cars back, in the other lane, was a shiny new truck. The driver was young and cleanshaven. I got a good look at him. Clearly Latino. And he seemed to be looking at Karen. I turned around quickly and ducked down.

"Go past our turn off and go right. Let's try to lose him."

She sped up and crossed over past our turn-off. She ran the stop sign at the bottom of the off ramp and turned right. The back tires slipped, but she regained control and accelerated.

I looked over my shoulder and the truck was just stopping at the bottom of the off-ramp. It turned right also.

Karen executed a left turn onto a small road and then another left into a little neighborhood. She pulled into any alleyway, stopped behind a dumpster and killed the engine. We both hunched down and waited. I risked a glance above the dashboard every minute or so. It was an exceptional dumpster. We saw no one except a kid who yelled, "Go for it."

We finally started up the car and drove home, looking both ways like good citizens. My hands were shaking as I tried to get the keys into the front door. I poured Karen a drink. It was a real test of my sobriety.

And then nothing happened.

Chapter 56

WE HAD BEEN HUNKERED down since the incident. Karen was having nightmares. I was wound up and wasn't getting a lot of sleep. We were both irritable and had been scraping little pieces off each other.

Sometimes, in the midst of a truly horrible situation, something wonderful happens. A small joy that is really a big deal.

And so it was Christmas, a small creature that came to our door unbidden. Over breakfast Karen told me it was Christmas Eve. I hadn't noticed.

We took the car into the mountains West of Santa Margurita There is a National Forest. The map showed that the only road goes to a campground that is closed all winter. Karen fell asleep after ten minutes. She was exhausted from the stress.

We wound through the hills on a crumpling two-lane road. There were no railings. A steep drop to the right leveled off into the vista of a long, pine-filled valley. From time to time, a stream glinted at us between the trees below.

I was driving slowly. As I came around a sharp curve I had to brake sharply as a red fox and her kits scampered across the road. Karen grumbled, but went back to sleep.

The air was fresh and cold. Fluffy clouds slowly wandered, like sheep, in the deep blue sky. I put down the windows a bit to let the wind blow in my hair. It gave Bruno the same idea and his head was lolling out the back window with his ears blowing back. Copy dog.

Karen stirred in the cold air. She shook off her sleep, put her hands on her arms and shook herself. "Brrr. That feels really good."

It took about an hour. Along a dirt road Karen found a miniature pine tree. I cut it. We collected boughs and pine cones and brought them home.

It was probably illegal, but, hey, I was working for the FBI. I knew they would stand behind me. They had been standing well behind me for months.

We made a little stand out of scrap wood. There were no ornaments. Just some pine cones and Karen's gold necklace. She had a little star shaped pin we attached to the top.

Karen cut strips of aluminum foil and we draped them around the limbs of our little tree. We put some of the pine cones and boughs around the bottom. I think it was the most beautiful Christmas tree I have ever seen.

We placed a few of the pine boughs in the middle of the dining room table around a candle, the end of which we had heated and anchored to a dish. The flickering candle shed its happy light over a simple meal.

After dinner, we sat on the floor in front of the tree and held hands. Bruno squeezed in between us. The flickering fire in the fireplace was the only light after our dinner candle had gutted out. Shadows played across the windows where the branches of the old oak tree in the yard danced with the wind.

The moon had always seemed timid in town, but out here it weighed down the sky, shining a cold radiance over the empty fields. It wasn't a white Christmas. But Jesus didn't have a white Christmas either.

Karen and I sang Christmas carols in bits and fragments or we just hummed to the accompaniment of the crickets. After a while, Karen put her head on my shoulder and we sat there in silence.

It was the best Christmas ever.

Chapter 57

"WHY DO YOU THINK he did it?"

It kind of came out of the blue a couple of days after Christmas. I was blindsided by a wave of anger at Willy. I had paused while lifting a fork full of spaghetti to my mouth. We were sitting at our little table in the kitchen with the mismatched chairs. Bruno sat under the table, attentive to the possibility of eating again. It was another grand night in Santa Margurita.

"Gosh, Jimmy, I don't know. Maybe you should start by defining 'he.'"

After almost a month, things were getting a bit testy. There is one thing about hiding out. You get to learn new things about your mate. I've learned, for instance, that Karen is a lousy shot. There are several bullet holes that will need patching before the owners inspect the house.

I love the woman. It's not just that she's beautiful and smart. There is a deep sensuality about her. She is a woman made for a rumpled bed. But there is one thing I've learned in my life. Sex is easy. Living together is hard.

Our life in captivity was made up of a hundred small repetitive moments. I'd taken to waking up each morning and rolling over to Karen and saying, "I'm sorry."

She always asks, "Why?" I think she does that to humor me.

"Just getting a jump on the day." To which she responds by punching me.

I would then roll out of bed and make up my side while she snuggled back under the covers. I brew the coffee. When the aroma filled the house, she would appear yawning and eager, holding out her cup.

After that, our days diverged. I spent a couple of hours at my computer scanning for news that might be important to us. All I got was news about the flu epidemic.

Karen would do her Pilates in front of her television instructor. I learned to hate that instructor's voice. Then we would plan lunch.

We ate lunch. Then we would plan dinner. We made dinner. We ate dinner.

After dinner, we would watch television. Santa Margurita has three channels. The FBI wouldn't spring for cable. I can tell you, the barn scene from *The Texas Chain Saw Massacre* is a masterpiece once you've seen it four times.

Finally, around nine we would trundle off to bed. Some days were better than others.

Repeat.

When the days are repetitive, they tend to merge into each other. We needed to really think about it to know what day it was.

Going out for a drive was a high point. If this goes on much longer, suicide will be redundant.

Maybe that's why this question bubbled up.

We were sitting in our tiny dining area in the kitchen. It was the sixth day in a row we were having some variety of pasta.

"I mean Willy. I don't understand why he did it. Why would he throw us under the bus? He knew he was in business with some really nasty people. He could have gotten us killed."

Karen was in sweatpants. I was wearing jeans and an old denim shirt that I had worn all week. I had a two-day stubble. She looked great. I looked like a derelict.

"I don't think we'll ever know for sure," Karen said. "We're talking about a dead man here. He's not likely to tell us."

"But it really bothers me. Willy wasn't a real friend," I said between chews. "But I thought he liked us."

"I think he did too."

"Then why did he do it?" I demanded.

She paused to consider that. Then she looked up with an expression of understanding in her eyes. Karen has an instinct for people.

"You know, Jimmy, I really don't think Willy ever meant to harm us. He was a little, innocuous guy. I think he just was in over his head."

Did she really believe that?

"Okay, maybe, but why did he involve me?"

I was happy to push my plate aside and ignore dinner. Karen, bless her heart, is a lousy cook. The only thing this pasta had that was related to al dente was the dent it was making in my stomach. Maybe I could sneak a snack later.

"This is only a guess. But I really think Willy respected you. He needed your help. Things were suddenly going too well. Willy never expected to be successful. The business was growing so fast. Lots of fast-growing businesses fail because they can't get the capital to keep up. I think he didn't know what to do. It scared him."

"But I don't know anything about business. Certainly not that business."

Karen lowered her head and put a knuckle to her lips in thought for a moment.

"Think about it, Jimmy. How many real people did Willy know? You're smart. You're articulate. Willy must have thought you were a genius."

Well, when you put it that way. Maybe she was right.

Her voice rose a little. "And remember, he never got you involved with the dirty stuff. The money laundering. That came in and went directly to him."

"Sure, but maybe he just didn't want me to know about it."

"Maybe. I'm speculating. But I think Willy hoped you'd be able to take over the company and make it profitable. Create a real business so he could keep the cartel out of his pants. He was going nuts trying to get everything done and still keep them happy. He couldn't let the business fail. He certainly didn't want them asking questions."

"You mean the skimming? I think that's what got him killed."

"Yes. But maybe he even saw the company as a way out."

"How?"

"The company was just window dressing to the cartel. A side-show to a very profitable enterprise. Maybe he hoped to put away enough to get away."

She spread her hands on the table in a gesture of uncertainty.

I simply nodded.

"Willy's real problem was that the business was going so well, it was absorbing money, not throwing it off," Karen said.

"You've said that twice. I don't get it. If the business was so suc-cessful, why didn't it gush cash?"

"We saw the same thing when we started the law firm, Jimmy. Don't you remember? We had to find clients. Then we worked for a month. We billed for the work. And no money came in. We had to wait sixty or ninety days or more for our clients to pay. It took six months for us to break even. We nearly starved."

"I do remember your nearly going nuts trying to pay a little bit on each of our bills. You seemed a bit stressed." Karen glared at me.

"We had to pay the rent and the secretary. Your malpractice in-surance. And our own bills. It was awful. We were going through the money we had saved so quickly."

I was oblivious to all of that.

"And we didn't even have to buy land, seeds, greenhouses and all the other stuff Wee Willy's needed, and wait for months before they grew anything. Even when the money finally started to come in it wasn't enough for all the additional employees Willy needed to run a growing business. And all the other extra costs of selling more products."

"Sure."

"All the cartel cared about was that the business break even so they could report the dirty money as income, pay the tax, and bingo, it was clean."

"But I still don't see it."

"Jimmy, I think Willy was a little guy looking up from the

bottom of a well he didn't even realize he'd fallen into. Maybe that's why he was high all the time."

I personally thought that was a bridge too far. Karen looked at me and sipped at her wine. She ignored the spaghetti. Smart girl.

A bead of sweat ran down my side. I got up to open a window. It was getting stuffy in the kitchen. A cool breeze touched me.

"Thanks," Karen said. She turned her face towards the window. "That feels good." A lock of hair fell into her face and she brushed it away.

"We didn't exactly do the job Willy hoped for, did we?" I said returning to my seat. Bruno shifted to make room for me. "Everything fell apart because I brought in Singer."

"That wasn't your fault. Wee Willy's was flat broke. You didn't have a choice."

"I guess so. Maybe if Willy hadn't been so high that day…"

"And if green were red."

"Huh?"

"It's a tautology. You know, something that is indisputably true. I remember that from my freshman English for some reason. Never mind."

"Okay. Maybe Willy was caught in the middle. I hope you're right. It's really kind of nice to think he didn't set us up."

Karen pursed her lips and sat up a little straighter as if something had clicked.

"I don't think he did, Jimmy. Actually, I think the opposite. Maybe we should feel sorry for the guy instead of being angry at him."

"That may be a bit more than I can swallow. Why, for goodness sake?"

"When things started to go bad, I think Willy felt awful about getting you involved. You remember, that's when he made his will. It's the only thing that makes sense. I think he left you everything he had to say 'I'm sorry.' It was the only gesture he could make to apologize."

Chapter 58

It was our last night in Santa Margurita. We were both played out with the tension.

"I want to have dinner somewhere," I said. "Anywhere. It's our last night. We'll go first thing in the morning. I've got to get out of the house tonight. I'm going out of my mind. And it's New Year's Eve."

"Jimmy, I don't think we should. There's too much going on."

"What are the chances someone will see us? And what can they do if they happen to? No one even knows where we live. If it looks bad, we can pick up Bruno and leave tonight. In fact, why don't we take Bruno with us."

"I guess," she said with a distinct lack of enthusiasm.

"I know what the guy looks like. I'll see him before he sees us."

It was a little unnerving. Scared wasn't in Karen's wheelhouse. She was scared.

"And a glass of Zager Chardonnay for my wife," I said. I'm an optimist. I was surprised at the wine list at the Old Mill. It was small, but surprisingly good. If the steaks were this good, I'd be a happy and well-fed man. I thought Karen was beginning to relax.

There were only two other couples in the restaurant. New Year's Eve wasn't their big night.

I was sitting facing the door. Karen was sitting to my left. Bruno was lying by my right shoe. Health laws were a little lax here in the country.

"You look wonderful this evening," I said.

The waiter delivered the wine and my sparkling water.

I lifted my glass. "Here's to going home."

Karen lifted her glass to toast. I spilled mine.

"Jimmy? What?"

I think my face went white. The Latino from the truck had just walked in the front door. He was wearing a suit and tie. He looked around and focused on Karen. Then he smiled.

He came slowly across the room towards us. Bruno lifted his head and growled. I stood up in front of Karen. I was tensing to launch myself at him if he made any move.

He reached into his jacket. I lunged forward with my fist raised.

His eyes widened. He pulled out his wallet.

I stood there with my fist back.

"Hi. I'm Carlos Santana," he said rather hesitantly. He pulled out a card and handed it to me. "I noticed your wife in town the other day."

"What do you want?"

"You're new in town, aren't you? I'm the local realtor. I thought you might need some help."

Chapter 59

IT WAS EARLY, BUT the conference room at Wee Willy's was bursting with activity. The chairs had been pushed back against the far wall. Three young lawyers shuffled around large square black briefcases.

They would dip into one, withdraw a stack of papers and examine them. Then they would carefully square the pages and place them on the conference table, lining them up neatly.

A folding table had been set up under the window. It was laden with fruit, bagels, cream cheese and Danish. John Campion was standing with a cup of steaming coffee in his hand. He was smiling down at Anthony Sturgis.

"Of course not," Campion said, gesturing with his cup. "We don't mind coming to you to get the deal closed. Let's make it happen."

Karen and I had returned the day after New Year's. Being still dead, I wasn't allowed in the room, but Sturgis had permitted me to sit with his technicians who were recording the closing for posterity and, hopefully, evidence in court. It had been a hectic few hours setting up the tiny mics and hidden cameras, but we had an unobstructed view of the proceedings.

The door opened and Clyde came into the room. He looked every bit the lawyer in his dark suit and blue tie. Sturgis motioned him over.

"I think you know Mr. Campion."

Campion did not look overjoyed to see Clyde. Just because

Clyde had told him to stick his job up his ass was no reason to hold a grudge.

"Clyde is representing us in the closing," Sturgis said.

"Clyde," Campion said coolly, putting out his hand. John Campion was a man who was used to getting his way and unpleasant when he did not. "I know you don't have a lot of corporate experience, but I'm sure my associates," he gestured towards them, "can give you all the help you need."

Nice going, John. And you did that with a smile.

Clyde broke into a big grin. "Why thank you, Mr. Campion. I'm sure I can learn a great deal here."

Campion hadn't expected that. Maybe the boy was dull. It might have been a good thing they passed on him.

It took over two hours to arrange the papers and another hour for Clyde to examine them. The bagels had been replaced by sandwiches and bags of potato chips.

Finally, Clyde looked up and said to Sturgis, "I'm okay with these."

John Campion got up from the chair he had been occupying and unfolded himself.

"It's been a long road, but here we are finally," he said addressing the room. "I want to thank Mr. Sturgis for his cooperation and support. I have to say, I have never seen a more thorough due diligence on my clients. You are an excellent chief financial officer, Mr. Sturgis, and a credit to Wee Willy's."

The Campion & Gilbert associates nodded and clapped. Sturgis looked mostly at his shoes and gave an "aw shucks" gesture although he did have a broad smile.

"Well, let's sign the documents and get this closed," Campion said, slapping Tony Sturgis on the shoulder. "I have been authorized by my clients to sign on their behalf." And he stepped to the table.

Signing twenty stacks of documents, each of which had five copies, would have discouraged lesser men. But eventually, Campion and Sturgis made their way around the table.

"There," said Campion, dotting the "i" on the last signature sharply.

"Finished." He shook a cramp out of his hand and screwed the cap back on his fountain pen.

"Can we transfer the funds now, Mr. Campion?" Sturgis asked.

"Normally, Tony, I would say you show me yours first." Campion grinned with a small laugh at his joke. "But this is a unique occasion."

He picked up the phone, dialed and gave a brusque order. "Call me," he said.

In five minutes, the phone rang. He picked it up and listened. "Done," he said.

"Now, Tony, except for your bonus check and severance, are we finished?" He extended an envelope to Sturgis. Sturgis opened the envelope and withdrew a check. He looked at the number and nodded.

"Thank you," Sturgis said replacing the check in the envelope and putting it in his inside jacket pocket. "Except for these, of course."

Sturgis reached down and extracted a small stack of papers from his briefcase. He smiled wolfishly as he handed them to Campion.

"Ah, and what is this?" Campion said. The smile slid from his face like a bird hitting a window.

"This is a subpoena," he said.

"And a search warrant."

"You can't subpoena my firm records. What is the meaning of this?"

"Mr. Campion, I have not been entirely honest with you. I am Special Agent Anthony Sturgis of the Federal Bureau of Investigation. We have reason to believe that your law firm is a party to an ongoing criminal conspiracy."

"This is outrageous. We have attorney-client privilege. We will fight this in court."

"I'm sure you will, Mr. Campion."

"When we are through with you, you won't be able to get a job as a security guard. I have many important friends."

"I am certain you do. I look forward to meeting them."

Campion stalked out of the room, slamming the door. His three associates looked at each other with their mouths hanging open. They hadn't realized yet that their ride home was gone.

Chapter 60

"THAT'S IT? YOU'RE JUST going to leave?"

It was the morning of the day after the closing. I was allowed to be alive again.

"What does it look like, Harris?"

I had walked into Wee Willy's as Sturgis was walking out hefting a box full of knick-knacks and personal photographs in both hands. He was dressed in his dark suit and starched white shirt.

He looked at me without much interest.

"It's been real and it's been fun, but it hasn't been real fun." He wasn't smiling.

"But what am I supposed to do with Wee Willy's?"

"I don't really care. This was an operation. We're done."

"But you didn't tell me you were leaving."

"I'll tell you the truth now, Harris. I don't report to you."

"But we're not prepared."

"Not my problem. I've got to deal with Mr. Campion and your law firm buddies."

That distracted me.

"You know they're not my buddies. What's going to happen to Campion?"

"I guess that will depend on what we find in his files and his personal accounts. But I'll bet he's in this up to his noodle. I hope they make pinstriped orange jump suits."

"But what about me?"

Sturgis made a dismissive gesture with his chin. His hands were full.

"I don't see you going to prison because of Wee Willy's. Unless of course there's something you haven't told me."

There was that.

"I didn't mean that. I meant the cartel."

"Oh, I think they will have bigger issues. I wouldn't worry about it. Unless, of course, you want to."

"Great. Can you at least put in a good word for me with the sheriff?"

"Now, Harris, I've told you before, we can't get involved in local affairs. Goodness, interfering in a murder investigation?"

"I didn't kill Willy."

"See, there's no reason I need to get involved."

"You didn't have any problem when you were trying to get me killed."

"Yes. But we needed you then. That was different. Oh, and for the record, don't expect us to pick up any more bills around here."

"What about my salary?"

"I'll bite. What about it?"

"Am I going to get paid?"

"Not by us. Besides, you were dead most of the time."

"I was still working."

"Bait doesn't work. It only sits and waits. Frankly, Harris, I hope never to see you again."

"That's not fair."

He shrugged indifferently.

"But you have to pay Clyde. You promised."

"And that I will. He is one fine lawyer. He did a hell of a job for us."

He walked out to his car and put the box on the roof. I walked after him. He opened the rear door without looking at me, grabbed the box and stuck it in.

As he got into the driver's seat, he turned and gave me a hard look before slamming the door. Then he was gone in a spray of gravel. My knees and my feelings were hurt.

I guess the government wasn't here to help me anymore. The place seemed very quiet. All the FBI agents had left the greenhouse.

It was only me and Valerie now. Sweet, loyal, transgender Valerie. Back after battling the flu to its knees.

"Hey, Valerie," I said, walking into the reception room.

"I quit," she responded.

"Valerie? What? Why are you quitting?"

"It's boring here," she said as she got up and grabbed her purse.

So, it was just me and several large boxes of money in small bills. Oh, well. I walked into my office and sat down.

And there in the middle of my desk was an order from the San Luis Obispo Superior Court setting the trial date for Kenneth Singer, et.al. vs. Wee Willy's Incorporated and James Emerson Harris.

So, let me recount here. The good news was that the cartel had bigger problems than me on their mind. And John Campion might join them in jail. In a cell with Manny Comacho, I hoped.

The bad news was that the FBI had left me twisting in the wind, Wee Willy's was broke and Kenneth Singer had resuscitated his law suit against me and Wee Willy's for $20,000,000.

My house had burned down. I was out of a job. And the police apparently still suspected me of killing Willy. I know because Sid was following me around again.

It was a perfect day.

Chapter 61

KAREN AND I WERE sitting in the bathtub in our room at the luxurious Hemmings Hotel and Marina on The Pointe in downtown San Buenasara. Luxury in San Buenasara is hot running water. Actually, it wasn't that bad.

My back was against the tub and Karen was leaning against my chest, cradled in my legs. Bruno was lying on the bathmat.

It had been a long day. Each of us had a wine glass. Karen was drinking Zager Chardonnay. I was drinking Welch's 100% Grape Juice.

I sipped it thoughtfully. It tasted like the '04.

12:04 p.m., the week before last. A great minute.

I'll say one thing for it. You could taste the grapes.

I had just gotten to the point of telling Karen that Valerie had quit and about the trial date for the lawsuit. She had her eyes closed and the water was still warm. I had my hands on her flat stomach. The view over her shoulder was starting to distract me, if distract is the word I'm searching for.

She opened her eyes and leaned her head back. "Not now, lover. We need to talk about completing Plan B."

I think she had a different Plan B in mind.

"Plan B?"

"You know, the plan to sell Singer Wee Willy's by threatening to file bankruptcy. We talked about it before the FBI got involved in trying to kill you. $2,000,000 in cash for the intellectual property?

We discussed it again right after Thanksgiving."

"Yes, I vaguely recall that." Actually, I had completely forgotten about it. Staying alive had focused my mind. Then a thought occurred to me. "You know, we could use all the money in the boxes to settle with Singer instead."

"Jimmy, that just doesn't feel right. We would still have Wee Willy's. We'd have to run it. And that money came from a lot of people who were hurting. It's dirty money."

I couldn't disagree, although I wanted to. She has high ethics. But money was involved here. I'm a lawyer.

Karen gracefully raised herself from the tub, pirouetting towards me. She grabbed a big towel and did one of those wrap things women know how to do. I felt a real sense of loss.

"Come on, we need to sit down and figure this out," she said stepping out. She grabbed another towel and wrapped her hair. I don't know where they learn to do that.

I rolled over on my knees and scrambled up using the sides of the tub. Karen handed me the last towel. I wrapped it around my waist. And it fell off. Finally, I just held the edges in place to sit on the couch in our so-called living room. Karen switched on the table lamp.

"Oops. Forgot my glass," I said lurching up. One doesn't abandon an '04 Welch's. "You okay?"

She had a pencil and paper out when I came back. She was holding the eraser against her lips, thinking.

"We need an outline of what to do," she said. "First, we need Clyde to redot all the i's and check all the t's on the intellectual property. It's been a while."

"We may have some new trademarks. Probably other stuff."

Karen scribbled a note.

"What about Wee Willy's Incorporated? Do we need to do anything with the corporation?" she asked.

"I think the corporation is dead. No one will want to touch it. Who knows what's under the rocks? Who even knows where the rocks are to look under? We'll have to sell the assets out of it."

"Can we?"

"What do you mean?"

"Do we own them?"

Now that was a nifty question.

"I think so. Wee Willy's is owned by a bunch of shell corporations. As far as we, or anyone else knows, Willy owned them. Maybe not, but I don't think anyone is going to step forward to dispute that."

"Okay," Karen agreed. "And you are Willy's sole beneficiary."

I leaned forward and put my glass of grape juice on the table. Then I leaned back into the corner of the couch and crossed my arms. I uncrossed my arms to pull the towel back around my waist. But I have great concentration.

"Yep," I said, undeterred. "And the sole officer of the company. So, yes, I think we can sell them."

"We still need Clyde to draft a bankruptcy filing."

"Right. I'll need that when I call Singer."

"When do we file?"

"I don't think we do. It's our leverage. And if Singer agrees to buy the assets for $2,000,000, forgives the loan and drops the lawsuit, we can pay off everyone. There's just one thing. I don't think I should be the one to call Singer. I think we have Clyde call and do the deal."

"Why? Are you afraid to call Singer?"

"I don't think he likes me. I'm not sure anybody likes me around here."

"Bruno likes you," she said.

"What about you?"

Karen stepped over and kissed me. Her towel came loose. I thought my Plan B was just grand.

Chapter 62

"Thank you for coming in, Mr. Harris."

"No problem, Sheriff. I appreciate your keeping me in the loop. I liked Willy." Well, kind of.

We were in the Sheriff's office in San Luis. The building was rather old, but her office was nice by police standards.

There was a metal desk and two metal chairs. But they had padded seats. The walls were green, but of a pastel shade. And there were big windows with a breathtaking view of the parking lot.

I had been surprised when she had called. She said she wanted to bring me up to date. I was pleased.

"This investigation has taken a long time," she said, with a bemused look on her face. "This case has just been one disaster after another. This flu thing has decimated our lab. For some reason, the FBI just wasn't responsive. Even the coroner was down and out, poor guy."

"Have you caught the killer?"

"We have. Finally."

"Who is he?"

She raised an eyebrow. "We haven't made an arrest yet. We need to wrap up some loose ends. For one, I have to get the statement you gave me on the record. I'd like to go over it with you."

"No problem."

"Do you mind if I record it?"

"No. Really, anything that will help. I'm tired of the San

Buenasara police following me around."

"Sorry about that, Mr. Harris. We'll see that it stops."

"Before we start, can I get you a cup of coffee? Anything?"

"Do you have a Diet Pepsi?"

She pressed a button and spoke into her phone. "Steve, would you please bring in a Diet Pepsi and a cup of coffee for me? You know how I like it."

It was nice that she said "please."

As her assistant brought in the drinks, she set a small oblong recorder on the desk between us. She turned it towards me and pushed the button.

"This is Sheriff Sylvia Patera. The date is January 10. I am speaking with Mr. James Emerson Harris." Then she pushed replay to check the recording and nodded with satisfaction.

"Okay, Mr. Harris. Let's go." She started the recorder again.

"Mr. Harris. You gave me a statement at the scene of the death of William Witkowski."

"Yes, I did."

"The purpose of this interview is to review and record that statement."

"Right."

"I have my notes, so I will ask you to repeat some facts you told me at that time."

She flipped through a pad on her desk.

"So, let me see… yes. During the time Mr. Witkowski was killed, you were at home."

"Yes."

"You had stayed at home from work both that day and the previous day."

"That's correct." I took a sip of the soft drink.

"And the woman with whom you live…"

I smiled as she tried to pin down the relationship and gave up.

"Karen Harris… It is 'Harris' isn't it, Mr. Harris? From a former marriage?"

"That's correct." As far as it goes.

"Ms. Harris was in and out of the house during that period, for an extended time in some cases."

"I don't know what you mean by extended."

"For example, she was out shopping and in your law office."

"Yes."

"And when you woke up at..." She paged through her notes. "Six-thirty in the morning on the day you discovered the body, she was gone."

"Yes."

"No one saw you or telephoned you and you did not make contact with anyone else during the times she was gone."

"Not that I recall."

"You had gone to work for Wee Willy's and you went up to see Mr. Witkowski about some financial problems you discovered. That is when you found the body."

I was aware of the door opening behind me and someone coming quietly into the room, but I didn't turn around. I wanted to concentrate.

"Did you know of these problems when you gave up your law practice to join the company?"

"No, I didn't."

"Didn't you feel betrayed by Mr. Witkowski?"

That surprised me.

"Didn't it anger you?"

"I wasn't pleased." And I wasn't pleased with the question either. I was getting a bad feeling. My throat was dry. I took another sip of the Diet Pepsi.

"How angry were you, Mr. Harris?"

"Wait a minute."

"Weren't you furious? Mr. Witkowski was destroying your life." She didn't wait for a response. "You were the sole beneficiary of his estate. Didn't you feel he owed you?"

"What are you talking about?"

Her voice rose and her tone was accusatory. "Mr. Harris, didn't you kill William Witkowski?"

"My God, no."

"We believe you did. We now have full lab reports. They are conclusive."

"I don't care what they say. I didn't kill Willy."

"Mr. Harris, there is no trace evidence in the house that links anyone else to the scene but you, other than the fingerprints of the maid. She can fully explain where she was during the critical hours."

"This is crazy. You can't believe this." My voice was rising.

"Yours are the only fingerprints on the weapon, other than Mr. Witkowski's. And you had his blood on your clothes."

"Of course my prints were on the screwdriver. I told you that." I was allowing my cool demeaner to slip and fall off the chair.

"There is not a single shred of evidence that anyone was in Mr. Witkowski's house other than you."

"That can't be true."

"We interviewed every person up and down the road. No one saw anyone come or go other than you."

"They had to be wrong."

"The ground was wet from the rain. We got good tire tracks from the mud on the road. We analyzed them. After we eliminate those from our vehicles, there were only two remaining, yours and the tracks from Mr. Witkowski's neighbor above him, where the road ends."

"Then it had to be them."

"They were on a cruise to Hawaii at the time of death."

"This is crazy. Someone must have walked in."

"There were no footprints in the ground. We checked. It was you, Mr. Harris. Why did you do it?"

"I didn't kill, Willy. I was the one who called the police."

"Maybe you got into an argument. Maybe it was an accident. Was it self-defense, Mr. Harris? Did you get scared? Now is the time to tell us the truth. It's the only way we can help you."

I jumped to my feet. My hand clinched and I involuntarily crushed the soda can. Drink spurted onto Patera's desk. She leaped back to avoid the puddle of soda, sending her chair skidding.

"I don't need your help. I didn't do it!"

Hands fell on my shoulders and pushed me back onto the chair.

"This is ridiculous. I demand you either charge me or let me go."

Sheriff Patera stepped around her desk.

"James Harris, I am arresting you for the murder of William Witkowski."

"What about the drug cartel?" I said weakly.

The Sheriff snickered. "That's a good one, Mr. Harris. You have the right..."

Right? How could it be so wrong.

Chapter 63

I'D NEVER BEEN IN jail. It's lonely and you don't meet the best people. It's certainly not where you want to spend your birthday.

Karen and Clyde came and brought me presents. They arranged for a turkey dinner. But we didn't sing songs or anything. On the other hand, it simplified my birthday wish.

My cellmate for the last three days had been moved into County Jail so he could appear for his trial for armed robbery, a crime for which he was absolutely and completely innocent. One good thing about being in here for murder, the other prisoners kept their distance and you could take a shower in peace.

Clyde had tried to get me out on bail. But the court ruled against me. Having such a dangerous lawyer loose in society offended the judge.

Karen came every morning. Since I didn't know how this happened, I couldn't explain it to her. I couldn't explain it to myself.

Clyde and I had spent two hours a day for the last ten days trying to set a strategy for my defense. If Clyde was a better lawyer, he'd go out and find the real murderer. It was difficult since there were no clues, but that shouldn't have stopped him if he were really dedicated.

"Damn it, Clyde, Willy got me into this mess. But I didn't kill him with a screwdriver. I'd have strangled him."

"Well, that's good to know."

"This isn't funny."

"Oh, right."

"We can make the point that Wee Willy's was broke and so was Willy. I had no motive."

"You didn't know that. Besides, I just sold Wee Willy's to Kenneth Singer for $2,000,000. $3,000,000, if you count the loan forgiveness."

I was becoming more and more desperate. I rose to my feet and started pacing the room, looking down at my shoes. Everything pointed to my being the murderer with a certainty that was hard to deny. I certainly didn't recall killing Willy. I looked up.

"Clyde, the murderer wore gloves and had shoes that didn't leave a mark."

"Sure, and wore a hazmat suit that didn't leave any DNA. Maybe he was dropped in from a helicopter. It seems like a lot of trouble to go to if the alternative was shooting him with a rifle."

"Yeah, it seems a little farfetched, doesn't it? A jury might not buy it."

"If I could sell that one..." He just stopped and shook his head in disgust.

"Maybe someone has figured out how to shoot a screwdriver a half a mile," I said.

"That one would be easier to sell."

Not only could Clyde not come up with a defense. This was going to be reflected in his yearly performance evaluation.

Two days later Clyde created another problem.

"Boss, Singer say he ain't gonna go through with the deal to buy Wee Willy's."

"What? Clyde, for $2,000,000 he's getting a bargain."

"That ain't the problem.

"He found out you in jail. The $2,000,000 be okay. He done even agree to pay our costs and attorney fees. He scared he won't get good title to them assets."

"Come on, Clyde, you can convince him."

"No, I cain't, Boss. He be right."

That was a surprise.

"What. Why not?"

Clyde reverted to his polished English.

"You're charged with murder.

"I remember."

"Murder, not manslaughter or some lesser crime."

"Clyde, what did you want me to do? Tell them it was an accident? I was holding the screwdriver and it slipped?"

"Well, that might have been a good idea. But, with a murder charge, we have a problem. You see, you can't inherit from the person you murdered."

"And our ownership is based on Willy's will."

"Right. It's how we made the sale and it was the basis of your right to vote to approve it."

"What do we do?"

"Other than prove you innocent, I have no idea." If Clyde didn't have an idea, how could I.

"Oh, good Clyde. I don't want to spend the rest of my life in prison and be broke too. So, what's our next step?"

"Got me."

———————

I had just finished lunch. The food wasn't as bad as you might have expected. Still, I can't say I'd call and make a reservation. I flopped back into my bunk and picked up the Reacher novel I was reading. Jack Reacher would have been out of this in 300 pages.

A guard lumbered up to my cell door. "Harris, up. The Sheriff wants to see you."

I struggled to my feet.

"Stand back," he said to my new cellmate.

He opened the door and I stepped out and extended both arms for the handcuffs I had worn every time I was out of the jail.

The deputy shook his head and pushed me in front of him. Odd. Maybe they were playing bad cop-worse cop.

He held open the door of the Sheriff's office. The Sheriff was waiting. There was a man in the room.

"This is Assistant District Attorney Bradley Winters," the Sheriff said gesturing to the man. "He's in charge of your case."

"I'm still not going to confess, Sheriff. I don't want to plea bargain. And I want my lawyer. So, let's get this over with quickly."

"Please, Mr. Harris, sit down."

I reluctantly took the seat she offered. She sat down behind her desk. Winters hovered.

"You won't need your lawyer."

"I will unless you intend to violate my Constitutional rights."

"Mr. Harris, I don't like you."

Join the club. I wasn't crazy about her either.

"But I owe you an apology. We... owe you an apology."

I was taken aback. "Apology?"

She looked up at the ceiling and sighed.

"Yes, we are dropping all charges against you. You are free to go."

"Wait a minute. What's going on here. Who killed Willy?"

"Well, Mr. Harris, it appears that Willy killed Willy."

"Take that from the top."

"We finally got the autopsy report."

"You didn't have an autopsy before you arrested me?"

"No, it was an unusual case. The report was delayed by the flu epidemic. The coroner was sick. It was such a clear case on the evidence that the District Attorney and I felt it was necessary for the public's safety that you be incarcerated."

Well shucks.

"What did Willy die of? Poisoning? Some infernal device? Aliens?"

"Mr. Harris, this is difficult for me. I know that you are known for your sense of humor, but please don't make this harder."

"So?"

"Mr. Witkowski died of a stab wound from the screwdriver you found."

"Then why are you letting me go?"

"The coroner concluded that from the angle of the wound and

the force necessary to drive in the screwdriver in order to leave the bruise marks on the skin from the handle, the perpetrator had to be a left-handed, weight-lifting midget. Or that Mr. Witkowski fell from a high surface onto it. Maybe his kitchen table tipped over when he was trying to fix the light. Maybe he was intoxicated."

Talk about falling on your sword. My mind flashed back to Willy lying on the floor of my office, gazing up at the ceiling after tripping over his own feet. Way to go, Willy, you poor, high, clumsy bastard.

Chapter 64

"Now wait just a second, Harris. That's the government's money. You can't keep it."

Oh, my life was better. I was out of jail and now I got to speak to Special Agent Sturgis again. But, this time, I had my trusty attorney, Clyde, by my side.

I took the lead.

"Sturgis…"

"That's Special Agent Sturgis."

I ignored him.

"You already got $27,000,000 plus whatever you got for your bonus and severance. You did turn your bonus over to the FBI, didn't you?"

"Fuck you, Harris."

"You said you were walking away. I could do anything I wanted to with Wee Willy's."

"Do you have that in writing? Any witnesses? That money is ours."

"I could sue you."

"Right And be in court for three years. No way you're going to do that. You'd lose anyway."

"Tony, this is Clyde," he said, interrupting before we came to blows.

"Oh, hi Clyde. What are you doing there? Not that it isn't great to talk to you."

"Great to speak to you too, Tony. How is the family?"

Huh, the family?

"Coming along."

"Tony, I'm representing Wee Willy's. I don't think we have a problem here."

"You don't. Why?"

"There's nothing left in Wee Willy's for you or anyone else. Under corporate law, the money the FBI paid to run Wee Willy's was the cost of a criminal investigation, not a loan. And even if it was, the Singer loan superseded it in time."

"We're not asking for a loan to be repaid. We want the $2,000,000 the assets were sold for as the fruit of a criminal enterprise."

"That's why I don't think there's anything to fight over. Wee Willy's paid off its vendors and filed all its back payroll tax returns. That cost around $700,000."

I had no idea where Clyde was going with this.

"Okay, I can see that."

"And Wee Willy's is obligated by law to pay its employees. William Witkowski was entitled to $200,000 in back pay. And he had a right to twenty percent of any sale, so that's another $600,000."

"He's dead."

"I know, but death doesn't negate his contract rights." Those claims went to Willy's estate. Clyde didn't feel it was necessary to mention I was Willy's heir.

"Then Jimmy is entitled to $200,000 in salary too."

"He was only there a couple of months."

"There was a minimum of a year in his contract, unless he was terminated for cause. And he's entitled to ten percent of the sale. That's $400,000. A total of $1,700,000.

"There's still $300,000."

"Tony, look, I'm sorry, but Wee Willy's has to pay the payroll taxes on all that. Then they have to pay to dissolve the corporation. I don't think there's a $100,000 left.

"Clyde, I don't want to repeat myself. Send the $100,000."

"Gee, Tony, the corporation is entitled to have a little left for contingencies. Unless, of course, you want to be responsible for any future claims."

Sturgis sighed. "Damn it, Clyde, I wish you would have come to work for me. I'm a lot more fun than the guy you're sitting with."

I've been insulted. I've been slandered. But I've never been so affronted. I have a great sense of humor.

"Thanks, Tony. I'll be in touch soon," Clyde said. He was smiling like the Cheshire Cat when he hung up the phone.

"How do you think Special Agent Clyde Johnson would sound?" He laughed at the look on my face.

Thank God it was over. We could finally relax and get on with our lives. I had a wedding to plan. Well, plans to agree to. Well, I had to show up.

Chapter 65

I<small>T WAS SPRINGTIME</small>. A<small>ND</small> in Cummings words, "The world was puddle wonderful," what with the spring rains that had soaked the ground in the last two weeks. The air was fresh and the hills were green. The birds sang in the trees. It was my wedding day.

We were gathered in the Bruno Harris Dog Park. You may think it strange to have a wedding in a dog park, but it was a very pretty dog park and Bruno insisted. It had been closed for the occasion by order of the mayor. And the city had done its annual maintenance the day before, so the park was pristine. I'd say 'no shit,' but that would be an awful pun.

Judge Wilma Hendricks had agreed to preside. She was one of our Superior Court judges. She and I go a long way back, which is to say she hates me. But she loves Karen.

Bruno Harris, for whom the dog park is named, had agreed to be the ring bearer and Karen's best man. Karen wanted him to be maid-of-honor, but he drew the line there.

It was a bare bones wedding. You know, limited to twenty close friends and a bowl of punch. Of course, there was the grand reception afterwards for 100 people, but who cares. It's only money.

Love may be wonderful the second time around, but let me tell you, it is even better when you're getting married to your first love. Again.

I told Karen, that given our history, I never wanted to hear out of her mouth the words, "What have I done." She's a smart lady. I'll bet there will be a work-around.

Okay, truth. I am a little nervous. I mean, who wouldn't be, dressed in a new blue, tailor-made suit and a red Hermes tie. I have only had one suit and I wear it to court and to funerals. Karen didn't think that suit was suitable.

We figured out what to do with the cartel's money. First, we counted what was left. It came to $974,000.

We couldn't give it back to the cartel. I wouldn't give it to the FBI. Karen wouldn't let us keep it. I thought about it. After all, I'm a lawyer. But Karen pointed out that, with my luck, I'd go to jail for tax fraud and she'd never see me again.

We made an anonymous donation to the San Buenasara Drug Rehabilitation Center. They said it was more than their annual budget. But that was after we gave a $50,000 gift to the city to maintain the Bruno Harris Dog Park in perpetuity.

We had rented a house up the street from The Lilly Pad so we could watch them rebuild our old house. The contractor promised me he wouldn't steal more than ten percent. Now that's the definition of an honest contractor.

And we got the law firm going again. We had all the money from my salary and bonus at Wee Willy's and Willy's money too that I had received as his sole beneficiary. And with all the money Clyde was earning doing legal work for the FBI, we were set for a while.

I did give Clyde a bonus for his work at Wee Willy's. It was a small bonus. After all, I brought in the job.

In any case, Clyde is now hard at work suing the County for wrongful imprisonment. Or, at least, he will be as soon as he has finished being my best man. He negotiated compensating time off.

I want him to hold out for an annual contract with the county for legal services. That should drive them nuts.

Karen says I can't have my big office back. She thinks Clyde deserves it. She did promise me a small office in the new house. But she put dibbses on it when she graduates law school in three years.

I was standing at the front of a red carpet laid out on the green grass. Judge Hendricks was beside me. She kept giving me dirty looks and shaking her head. The sky was as blue as I've ever seen it. There were some puffy white clouds in the Western quadrant, just as Karen requested. She has a great relationship with God.

Polly, who runs our local adult book store, started to play the Bridal March on his guitar, the one with the phallic symbols inlaid on the handle in mother of pearl. Lilly joined him on the flute.

Karen started down the aisle with Bruno at her side. She was holding a small bouquet of roses in front of her.

I hadn't seen her for a whole day. She insisted on staying in a hotel the night before. I mean alone. I mean, good grief, we had been married before. We had been sleeping in the same bed longer than I can remember at my age. Women.

But, my woman, thank goodness. I am blessed by her lack of judgement. She looked incredible in her tailored suit. The polka dots matched her eyes. Her red hair rippled in the light breeze. She may be the most beautiful woman I have ever seen.

She stopped beside me. Bruno, bless his heart, stopped too. After all, he had the pouch around his neck with the ring in it. I reached down. When I got up again, Karen was looking into my eyes. I've never been happier.

"Do you..." Judge Hendricks started.

And we are going to live happily ever after, at least until I screw up again.

Acknowledgements

First, and always, to my dear wife and partner, Anne. She has read and corrected this book as many times as I have, but with far more insight. I have been blessed all my life with the lack of judgment of beautiful women. I still am. Anne makes my life fun.

It is said that it is better to remain silent and be thought a fool than to speak and remove all doubt. This book would have removed all doubt if it had not been for my friend, Dr. Paul Tucker.

Paul was the Paul Hayes Tucker Distinguished Professor of Art at the University of Massachusetts, Boston, (a chair created in his honor) and is a renowned art scholar. I admire him, as I do all of my successful friends who graduated from Yale, for their ability to overcome their educational deficiencies. Of course, he went to Williams as an undergraduate.

I would have come a cropper many a time if it hadn't been for Paul's knowledge. He corrected me and challenged me. He did it in detail and he was always right. Dang it. Any errors left over are mine, not his, I assure you. I am fortunate to have him as my friend.

Micalyn Harris has read all my books. Her thoughts and insights are always helpful. Her questions make me think. This book is better because of her. And what fortitude. She keeps coming back.

Elaine Kendall was a saint and a very well read one at that. Elaine, among other things, taught me the difference between "shamble" and "shambles".

And finally, but not at all the least, to Noah benShea, my wise buddy who graces me with his knowledge. Bless him.

www.ingramcontent.com/pod-product-compliance
Lightning Source LLC
Chambersburg PA
CBHW031222260626
47169CB00007B/2149